THE MUNCHKINS REMEMBER

The Wizard of Oz
and
Beyond

Stephen Cox

E. P. DUTTON NEW YORK

This book is dedicated to my little friend
with a big heart, Mickey Carroll—
one of the Munchkins. Without him,
I couldn't have written the book.

*Published in the United States by E. P. Dutton,
a division of NAL Penguin Inc.,
2 Park Avenue, New York, N.Y. 10016.*

Published simultaneously in Canada by Fitzhenry and Whiteside, Limited, Toronto.

Library of Congress Cataloging-in-Publication Data

*Cox, Stephen, 1966
The Munchkins remember.
1. Motion picture actors and actresses—United
States—Biography. 2. Midgets in motion pictures.
3. Wizard of Oz (Motion picture) I. Title.
PN1998.2.C69 1989   791.43'028'0924 [B] 88-33438*

ISBN: 0-525-48486-8

Designed by Steven N. Stathakis

1 2 3 4 5 6 7 8 9 10

First Edition

Contents

CONTENTS

vi

Photo sections follow pages 6, 38, and 70.

Foreword

I was too young to perform in *The Wizard of Oz*, but it is a great pleasure to write this foreword, because I feel this motion picture opened a window to the real world for Little People.

For the first time, an opportunity was afforded Little People, or midgets as they were called, to act independently as people, not freaks. Most Little People were told when, what, and how to dress, eat, act, and talk—essentially how to live. Of course, there were exceptions, but very few.

This movie gave the actors a chance to run the gamut of emotions, from slapstick comedy to pathos. Steve Cox has done an excellent job of following the lives of the Munchkins during and after *Oz*.

Even today, thousands of Little People are still searching for the independence which is every citizen's heritage. In 1957, I founded Little People of America, Inc., to help persons of small stature attain that goal and accept the unique challenge of being a Little Person.

In 1975, I augmented this endeavor by founding the Billy Barty Foundation. Through fund-raising events such as the Billy Barty Little People Celebrity Golf Classic (now in its sixteenth year), we raise money that is channeled into medical research, educational scholarships, and the breaking down of attitudinal and architectural barriers that affect Little People.

Let freedom ring!

Billy Barty

BILLY BARTY

Acknowledgments

*"We thank you very sweetly,
for doing it so neatly."*

The author wishes to express his heartfelt gratitude to the following people and organizations, who gave of their time and energy for this book:

The Academy of Motion Picture Arts and Sciences, the Associated Press (Laurie Dodge), Mary Balzer, Diana Brown, Mark Collins, Robert Drake, Tom Forrester, John Fricke, Mark Gilman, Joanne Gregorash, Paul Henning, Pat Jordan, Tiney Kirk, Allen Lawson, John Lofflin, Tod Machin, Doug McClelland, Richard Mikell, Mary Ministeri, Anna Mitchell, Jean Nelson, Lillian O'Docharty, Jack Paar, Patty Reeder, Mary Ellen St. Aubin, Joseph Simms, Beverly Smith, Thom and Diana Storey, Rhys Thomas, Turner Entertainment, Edna Wetter, and my hometown pal Elaine Willingham, who prodded me to write this book.

Of course, a big round of applause for the thirty-one Munchkins whom I interviewed. My editor, Jeanne Martinet,

ACKNOWL-
EDGMENTS

x

deserves praise for her editorial guidance, professionalism, and enthusiasm. Others who were of enormous help in preparing the book for publication include Trent Duffy of Dutton and Susan M. S. Brown, my copy editor. And many thanks to my parents, Gerald and Blanche Cox, for their assistance in a variety of ways. Also to my sisters, Bernadette and Michele, and brother, Brian, who rooted for me when *The Wizard of Oz* aired opposite "Little House on the Prairie"—our dad's choice. He gave in.

Introduction

A book about a ten-minute scene in a movie? Preposterous! Why would anyone want to read a book just about the Munchkins?

The answers are simple.

In 1978 *The Wizard of Oz* was voted the third best film ever made by the American Film Institute. Moviegoers for the last half century have labeled it an ultraclassic, and the applause for the film still resounds through theaters and living rooms every year. Today the Munchkins are the only surviving cast members of the movie, and it's finally their turn to claim some of that applause.

Their scene, which is a spectrum of colorful imagination, has been embedded in the minds of young and old as one of the most enchanting sequences ever encased in celluloid. Indeed, affection for the Munchkins hasn't diminished, and their contribution deserves recognition. This is why I undertook the writing of the Munchkins' memoirs. It was no small task, believe me.

INTRODUCTION

2

The search for the Munchkins started with my favorite Munchkin right in my hometown of St. Louis. His name is Mickey Carroll, and we've been the best of buddies since I was little. Like a lot of the Munchkins, he still receives fan letters from all over the country. With a Munchkin in my own backyard, my starting point was obvious. But tracking down the rest of the surviving individuals who played Munchkins in the 1939 Technicolor dream was more difficult. To date, I have located only twenty-eight survivors of the legendary little people (one of whom has since passed away) and three of the children who portrayed Munchkins.

Munchkins seem to live in clumps. (There is such a thing as a peck of flour, a flock of geese, and, yes, that's right, a clump of Munchkins, it seems.) There was a clump of eight in the Los Angeles area, another clump in the Phoenix area, and a third in Florida. The rest of those who played Munchkins are scattered around the United States. Some remained in show business, and some had more conventional careers.

After spinning the wheels of the Munchkin network, I found that some of the little people kept in touch with others, thus my yellow brick road was ahead—albeit in desperate need of paving.

One Munchkin led me to another and so on. With the help of some very patient little people, such as Margaret Pellegrini—who has the memory of a wizard—hundreds of phone calls, and a few favors begged here and there, I met as many of these wonderful little people as possible. My only disappointment is that I couldn't have begun this book years ago; if I had, I would have been able to locate and meet more of these special people.

I was off to see the Munchkins, the wonderful Munchkins of Oz. And what a delight it was to meet such a conglomeration of people, with many views of the film, their scene, and its success. These little people are truly remarkable. An era will vanish when the last Munchkin goes to that Emerald City in the sky. *The Wizard of Oz* was the cause of the biggest and most successful grouping of these people in one place. It will probably never happen again in the history of humankind: proportionately correct midgets are a rarity today because of advances in hormonal treatments.

So get ready to take a trip that will bring you into the late 1930s, when show business was not a snow business. It was magic. It was hard work. It was fun. It was what Munchkinland was all about—fantasy.

Munch away!

1

"But If You Please, What Are Munchkins?"

In mid-November of 1938, a special group of people ambled their small-scale statures through the gates of Metro-Goldwyn-Mayer studios. These petite people, nearly 125 of them, were blatantly staring at the studio surroundings as much as the actors, technicians, and studio employees were gawking back at them.

"Acquired from 29 cities in 42 states," as an M-G-M press release stated, this bunch of diminutive people converged on the lot to make a movie that would mark their lives forever.

This was no ordinary motion picture, it was *The Wizard of Oz*. And they were about to become Munchkins.

The story involving Dorothy and her adventures was the inventive product of writer L. Frank Baum in 1900. Baum decided to bring Dorothy to a land called Oz after glancing at his file cabinet, with drawers marked "A–N" and "O–Z." The result of that little peer over his shoulder became an obsession for many readers as well as viewers of what is now a movie classic.

Since the movie's release in 1939, *The Wizard of Oz* has become one of the most revered stories ever shared by audiences.

It has been called America's favorite fairy tale. Some say it is timeless, others claim its appeal is in the underlying theme: "There's no place like home." Whatever the reason—and there are many—children everywhere have grown up loving one particular portion of the movie.

The colorful entrance into the fantasy world of Oz, which introduces the Munchkins, seems to be for children the most enchanting and cherished scene. It takes place beyond the rainbow, and it's what pleasant dreams are made of. It is also the first color scene in the film. Intently, focus is zeroed in on the whirlwind music and the little dwellers, who delightfully somehow match the height of young ones. With equal intensity, children's emotions shift to fear in the same scene when the most horrid of witches makes a sudden intrusion. For children, this is a tense moment. For most adults, it is a memory of their initial discovery of the enjoyment of movies.

Many viewers have grown up seeing this movie annually and anxiously anticipating its arrival on prime-time television; it is through this periodic showing that new generations grow to love the classic. The movie has been shown on television since 1956 with surprisingly good ratings. But what ever happened to the Munchkins? Nobody knew. For decades they have been caught in the American imagination, waiting to be rescued at just the right moment.

The word *Munchkin* seems to be forever instilled in our minds as denoting something tiny, wee, or miniature. This term, which Baum coined, has been used for so long it almost doesn't require association with the movie to be recognized as standing for one thing: little people. What isn't little is the appeal of these tiny charmers from Oz.

Ironically, just months before the classic convergence of more than one hundred midgets in Culver City, California, for the making of *The Wizard of Oz*, many of the very same people had acted in a "terror-ble" motion picture, *The Terror of Tiny Town*. It was a tiny success of an idea that really did more to make fun of midgets than it did to entertain. An all-midget musical western produced by Jed Buell in May 1938, the movie has, in fact, been cited many times in lists of the all-time worst films.

These actors traveled the spectrum, appearing in one of the worst films ever produced and, in the same year, one of the best. In between, and afterward, these little people carried on much the same lives as any other individuals. Some went on to careers in the entertainment industry. Others retreated to their homes and followed in family footsteps. Still others married, after meeting their spouses on the set of *The Wizard of Oz,* and rode into the Munchkin sunset.

What an achievement this was, to put together such a group of pocket-sized people from all points of the globe. It was the duty, by contract, of Leo Singer. He organized the Munchkin search and finalized the details surrounding collection of the little people for filming. It was a job that, although it paid him handsomely, was a test of Singer's patience and was his full-time employment for more than two months.

Singer, who had the master contract with Loew's, Inc. (Metro-Goldwyn-Mayer), was in charge of locating the little people and offering the roles to them. His quest was to sign 124 proportionately correct midgets for the movie, and this he accomplished, with nearly complete success. It is not known whether exactly 124 midgets walked onto the set, but records do confirm 122, plus nearly one dozen children. Collectively, they were just about 135, with one or two midgets leaving for differing reasons. (M-G-M memos show Munchkin Elsie R. Shultz leaving midway through filming because of an automobile accident, and an underage midget, Margie Raia, was found out and asked to exit Oz.) Unfortunately, M-G-M's complete records for such productions have since been disposed of, leaving only bits and pieces of documentation for even their most successful motion pictures.

For nearly seven weeks, between November 11 and December 28, 1938, this group of little people spent their daytime hours on a massive, beautifully decorated soundstage. They spent Thanksgiving and Christmas in Southern California, away from home, as they wrote to their families of their experiences. It was an adventure that can only be dreamed of now. It's only imaginable—and, on the screen, partly viewable. But the unpolluted legend left behind is in the minds of a privileged few. Luckily, the "little ones" have big hearts and are happy to share.

One of the most elaborate sets built for a movie at the time, Munchkinland is also one of the most memorable. (*Courtesy of National Screen Service, Inc.*)

WARDROBE STILLS

PROD 1060

MAYOR

CHAS BEGKE

OPPOSITE: The one and only mayor of Munchkinland, Charley Becker, displays his costume in this rare wardrobe test still. Becker, who is wearing his own spectacles and no makeup, has remained one of the most popular of all the Munchkins. LEFT AND CENTER: Two of the twenty-five Munchkin soldiers, Willi Koestner and Jakob Hofbauer. RIGHT: Matthew Raia poses in this wardrobe still in his City Father costume. *(All courtesy of the Academy of Motion Picture Arts and Sciences)*

The famous Lollipop Guild—the wardrobe blackboard in this original still calls them the 3 Little Tough Boys. Left to right: Harry Doll, Jerry Maren, and Jackie Gerlich. *(Courtesy of the Academy of Motion Picture Arts and Sciences)*

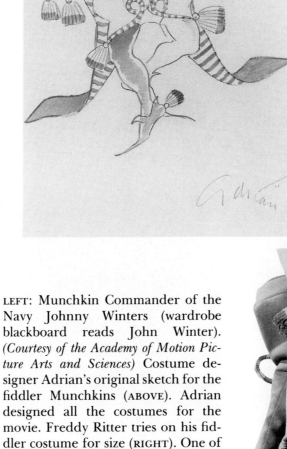

LEFT: Munchkin Commander of the Navy Johnny Winters (wardrobe blackboard reads John Winter). *(Courtesy of the Academy of Motion Picture Arts and Sciences)* Costume designer Adrian's original sketch for the fiddler Munchkins (ABOVE). Adrian designed all the costumes for the movie. Freddy Ritter tries on his fiddler costume for size (RIGHT). One of five red-and-white-striped Munchkins, Ritter dances behind Dorothy as she exits Munchkinland. *(Sketch courtesy of the Joseph Simms Adrian Collection, photo courtesy of the Academy of Motion Picture Arts and Sciences)*

ABOVE: Wardrobe still for Munchkin townsmen. Left to right: Lajos Matina, Joseph Koziel, and Tommy Cottonaro. *(Courtesy of the Academy of Motion Picture Arts and Sciences)* OPPOSITE TOP: The cast of the ultraflop *The Terror of Tiny Town*, an all-midget western musical, rode daily from Hollywood to the Lazy A Ranch, forty miles away, to shoot their movie. This was just months before they would film *The Wizard of Oz*. *(Courtesy of Joe Herbst)*

BELOW LEFT: On their way to Hollywood, a group of midgets from the Harvey Williams company stops to relax in the Midwest. Back row, from left: Emil Kranzler, Carolyn Granger, Matthew Raia, and Hildred Olson. Front row: James Hulse, Lewis Croft (playing the guitar), Alta Stevens. Harvey Williams in doorway. *(Courtesy of Ruth Robinson Duccini)* BELOW RIGHT: Little Billy Rhodes, Nita Krebs, and Billy Curtis pose for a picture on the set of *The Terror of Tiny Town*, May 1938. All three eventually became Munchkins. *(Courtesy of Nita Krebs)* BOTTOM: Some of the forty midgets used in *The Terror of Tiny Town*, on the set at the Lazy A Ranch in the Santa Susana Mountains, where exteriors were shot. *(Courtesy of Johnny Leal)*

ABOVE LEFT: Leo Singer with three of his Troupe, at Treasure Island at the 1939 World's Fair, San Francisco. Singer stands beside an unidentified woman companion. In the front, from left: Nita Krebs, Christie Buresh, and Jakob Hofbauer. *(Courtesy of Nita Krebs)*. ABOVE RIGHT: Papa Singer, they called him. Baron Leo Singer held the master contract with M-G-M to obtain midgets for *The Wizard of Oz. (Courtesy of Margaret Pellegrini)* LEFT: Artist's rendering of Papa Singer and two of his midget troupe, which appeared in the *San Francisco Chronicle* on August 2, 1939.

LEO SINGER

IRVING SINCLAIR
39

ABOVE LEFT: One of the smallest of the Munchkinettes, Hildred Olson from Dassel, Minnesota, illustrates her height by standing in front of a guitar case. (*Courtesy of Margaret Pellegrini*) ABOVE RIGHT: A group of midgets from the Henry Kramer troupe, which performed around the country. In the prejudiced era of the 1930s, the studio did not want any black midgets in *The Wizard of Oz*. Crawford Price (far right) is the only one in this photo who was not hired to be a Munchkin. (*Courtesy of Harry Monty*)

BELOW LEFT: The married Munchkins on the M-G-M back lot. The husbands stand behind their wives. Left to right: Henry and Dolly Kramer, Charles and Jessie Kelley (who, interestingly enough, later married Charley Becker), Johnny and Marie Winters, Prince and Ethel Denis, and Harvey and Grace Williams. (*Courtesy of Margaret Pellegrini*) BELOW RIGHT: Lady Munchkins on the back lot during a break in filming in December 1938. Back row, from left: Gladys Allison, Ruth Smith, Lida Buresh, Josefine Balluck, Lillian Porter, Gladys Wolff. Front row: Leona Parks, Margaret Nickloy, Freda Besky, Jeane LaBarbera, Margaret Williams, Christie Buresh, Helen Royale. (*Courtesy of Margaret Pellegrini*)

LEFT: The Culver Hotel, just blocks away from the studio, where most of the midgets lived during the making of *Oz*. Fifty years later, the building still stands, housing some offices. (*Photo by Stephen Cox*)

Shooting the scene: An M-G-M photographer catches a rare glimpse of dancing Munchkins. *(Copyright 1939 Loew's, Inc., renewed © 1966 by M-G-M)*

A rare photograph taken December 27, 1938, of some Munchkins on the back lot. Left to right: Prince Denis, Margaret Nickloy, Hildred Olson, Ethel Denis, and Johnny Winters. *(Courtesy of Margaret Pellegrini)*

TOP: The Lullabye League. Left to right: Nita Krebs, Olga Nardone, and Yvonne Moray welcome Dorothy to Munchkinland. *(Copyright 1939 Loew's, Inc., renewed © 1966 by M-G-M)* ABOVE: In this rare snapshot outside Stage 27, Meinhardt Raabe, Prince Denis, Matthew Raia, and Robert Kanter show off their costumes. *(Courtesy of Ruth Robinson Duccini)* RIGHT: Some of the little people also put on Winged Monkey costumes and swooped down after Dorothy and Toto. *(Copyright 1939 Loew's, Inc., renewed © 1966 by M-G-M)*

OPPOSITE TOP: Munchkin Mickey Carroll looks into the camera while waiting to shoot the next set of close-ups. Little Jeane LaBarbera (left) peers at Mickey. *(Courtesy of Mickey Carroll)* LEFT: Munchkin friends. Left to right: Ike Matina, Freda Besky, Ruth Smith, and Mike Matina. Ike and Mike were twins who had a reputation for hitting the bottle often during the production. *(Courtesy of Beverly Smith)* ABOVE: Glinda, the Good Witch of the North, introduces the dwellers of Oz to Dorothy. From the extreme right peeks Fern Formica, and next to Dorothy's hand is Little Olga Nardone, with Margaret Pellegrini directly above her. *(Courtesy of Tod Machin; copyright 1939 Loew's, Inc., renewed © 1966 by M-G-M)*

OPPOSITE TOP: With little W. H. O'Docharty in back and George Ministeri driving the coach, Dorothy gets whisked to her welcome at the Munchkin City Hall. (Courtesy of Tod Machin; copyright 1939 Loew's, Inc., renewed © 1966 by M-G-M) OPPOSITE: Some of the Munchkin men on the back lot. Back row, from left: Joseph Herbst, W. H. O'Docharty, John Bambury, unidentified, Charles Kelley, George Ministeri, unidentified, Carl Stephan, Walter Miller. Front row: Little Billy Rhodes, Charley Royale, Jerry Maren, Harry Klima, Freddy Ritter, and Henry Boers. (Courtesy of Pat Jordan) ABOVE: "From now on you'll be history . . ." Munchkins in view (left to right): Jack Glicken, Johnny Winters, Meinhardt Raabe (holding the death certificate), Little Billy Rhodes as the barrister, Charley Becker as the mayor, Matthew Raia, and soldier Jakob Hofbauer. (Copyright 1939 Loew's, Inc., renewed © 1966 by M-G-M)

TOP: The Lollipop Guild rehearsing, without the lollipop. "I wanted to keep that lollipop [as a souvenir], but I couldn't," says Jerry Maren (middle). *(Courtesy of Jerry Maren)* ABOVE: The studio pass issued to Munchkin Mickey Carroll so that he could step through the M-G-M gates for work each day. RIGHT: An amiable Charley Becker in 1939. *(Courtesy of Margaret Pellegrini)*

"We got a call to make a movie at a studio," says Munchkin Jerry Maren. "Not just *any* studio, it was the biggest studio in the world! Just to go through the gate was a thrill. I thought, 'Wow, I'm a movie star!'"

This would not be the last time Gerard Marenghi—who simplified his name to Jerry Maren—would walk through studio gates. As one of Hollywood's most successful midget actors, he is now semiretired, with a long career on which to reflect. But in that November of 1938, he was one of many.

For more than one hundred midgets to assemble in one place— for almost two months—marks history in and of itself. It is highly unlikely that a grouping of this nature will ever happen again, because 98 percent of these little people had a rare genetic makeup. They were midgets, not dwarfs, semishort people, or others. There is a difference, and M-G-M knew it.

The studio specifically wanted their Munchkins to be proportionately correct midgets, not dwarfs (although many times dwarfs are mistakenly called midgets in reference to their height, not their medical class). Since midgets have bodies that are proportionately correct, only in miniature, they are physically more adept at dancing and moving exactly as average-size people do than dwarfs are. Leo Singer was used to working exclusively with midgets, so he ultimately chose certain midgets in his search around the United States for M-G-M. Dwarfs are a separate classification of little people.

Although all adults of such size (no more than four and a half feet) are politely called little people; dwarfs differ from midgets because of their disproportionate body makeup. Sometimes their heads are somewhat oversize, or their trunks or arms are smaller or unusually larger. Dwarfs are shaped differently than proportionately correct midgets, but one thing both groups have in common is their height.

There were, actually, a handful of dwarfs used in *The Wizard of Oz*. Ruth Smith from Marshalltown, Iowa, Gladys Al-

THE
MUNCHKINS
REMEMBER

lison from St. Louis, and Johnny Pizo and Elmer St. Aubin were all dwarfs, though under their colorful, elaborate costumes they are not readily distinguishable from the rest of the Munchkins.

The defect causing unusual lack of height lies in a few different areas of the body. The pituitary glands malfunction at some point in gestation. Another explanation for some little people is their defective cartilage growth (achondroplastic dwarfism). Of course, the parents' genes also have an effect on growth. Reportedly, there are more than one hundred different defects causing the bone dysplasia that results in less than average height.

Because of advances in hormonal treatment, proportionately correct midgets are now very rare, and they may cease to exist in another fifty years, since many can be made to grow with hormone injections even into their twenties and thirties. Oddly enough, many of the midgets who performed in *The Wizard of Oz* grew a few inches when well into adulthood, without the aid of any hormones.

Therefore, the group assembled at M-G-M was remarkable not just because of their visual impact. Most likely, this special sector of the human race will never reappear again. *The Wizard of Oz* truly made the best of the little people's juncture; it is captured on film for posterity.

More Than a Handful

2

FOLLOW THE YELLOW BRICK ROAD

Legend has it that M-G-M wanted nearly three hundred midgets to portray Munchkins in their tale of a little girl who gets lost in a Technicolor dream. Whether this idea was actually attempted is not known. What is known and verified by contracts is that M-G-M's agreement with an agent named Leo Singer was to "procure and supply" the services of 124 midgets for their "photoplay" *The Wizard of Oz.*

"For more than 40 years, Singer has made the little things count," read the headline of a 1939 feature story about the agent in the *San Francisco Chronicle.* He put his little clients in show business and in one of the film classics that has sustained generations of audiences, with no end in sight.

Baron Leopold Von Singer (who legally signed his name "Leo Singre") was the leader of the midget entertainment world in the days of vaudeville. A German Jew born in Vienna, he traveled with fifty midgets throughout Europe and on to South America, Asia, and Australia, finally landing the group in the United States. During their travels abroad, the troupe of entertainers attracted other little people, so that eventually Singer had recruited a melting pot of the small performers.

To further clarify Singer's intentions, it must be mentioned that, unfortunately, midgets born in Europe in those days were very much looked down upon (no pun intended). For instance, according to one foreign little person, back in the 1930s Europe had many farms, and if a son or daughter couldn't work, he or she was considered somewhat of a family nuisance or an outcast. The United States, the land of opportunity, seemed to have much more to offer little people. Singer recognized this fact and gathered midgets to work for him in the entertainment world—many times regardless of their talent or lack thereof. Often the midgets didn't need to be talented; their size itself was enough. In those days, unfortunately, this spectacle was accepted, and they were exhibited just like freaks in a sideshow or carnival.

Singer was a wealthy man, comfortably chauffeured in his seven-passenger Lincoln limousine. Regarded as one of the richest men in New York, according to many of his troupe, he felt the fall keenly when he eventually lost much of his wealth in the stock market and a web of faulty investments. He died a pauper in the late 1950s.

To his midgets, he was known as "the boss" or "Papa Singer," titles he delighted in. He always loved commanding their respect. On October 1, 1938, Papa Singer signed the master contract with Metro-Goldwyn-Mayer to supply the Munchkins for their film. He was also employed by the studio to assist in the managing ("handling," as M-G-M's contract stated) of the midgets during the term of their own contracts.

This was not the first film endeavor for Singer's Midgets. Months earlier his group of little people and several independent performing midgets worked in an all-midget musical western film, *The Terror of Tiny Town*. For this project, Singer supplied nearly twenty of the forty midgets, who earned approximately $150 each for twelve days of shooting.

Singer began his work on M-G-M's Oz project in early September, when he scouted for midgets with the aid of several agents throughout the country. For this, Singer was paid $100 per week until October 3, after which he was to receive $200 per week until the full contract and his duties came to term. In early October, Singer was to travel from Los Angeles by train to the East Coast and then gather his little performers while trekking back to the West Coast.

On October 1, 1938, Loew's vice president, Eddie Mannix, signed his name in green ink while Leo Singer penned his signature in black on three copies of an eight-page contract. The notary public impressed a seal on each page while Singer and Mannix shook hands, and the official agreement was final. The Munchkins were to arrive November 11, ready to work. Two-thirds of the little people arrived on schedule; the rest trickled in daily until the last one expected, Bill Giblin, arrived on November 24. Those disembarking from a train that had brought them from all sections of the country were greeted at the depot by Leo Singer's limousine, his private chauffeur (a black man named Oscar Long), and a midget representative.

"When me and another midget, Leona Parks, stepped off the train, there was little Freddy Ritter waitin' for us," says Munchkin Margaret Pellegrini. "He was all dressed up and had Singer's limo there for us. I thought that was great treatment."

Twenty-eight midgets boarded a chartered bus from All American Bus Lines in New York. The bus began traveling the primitive roadways on the morning of November 5, en route to Los Angeles. As stipulated in the agreement with the bus line, meals and lodgings were provided, "not to exceed 25 cents for breakfast; 30 cents for luncheon and 40 cents for dinner . . . hotel accommodations for 5 nights at an average estimated at $1.00 per night, per person."

The trip landed the group in Los Angeles late in the evening of November 10; they were dropped off at the Adams Hotel or (most of the group) the Culver Hotel, both near the studio. The bus driver helped the exhausted yet excited little people handle their baggage. The lobby of the Culver Hotel suddenly

Culver City, California
October 1, 1938.

Loew's Incorporated,
Culver City,
California

Gentlemen:

I hereby warrant to you that I have entered into
a contract of employment with Leo Singer, whereby I have
agreed to render my exclusive services for you in connection
with the production of your photoplay "WIZARD OF OZ". I agree
that in rendering such services I will carry out such instruc-
tions as you may give me, and will perform all services which
may be required by you conscientiously and to the full limit
of my ability and as, when and wherever you may request. I
further agree to observe all of your studio rules and regulations.

I agree that I will look solely to Leo Singer for
all compensation for the services which I am to render for you,
and will not look to you or seek to hold you liable or responsi-
ble for the payment of any such compensation.

I hereby confirm the grant to you contained in the
agreement between you and Leo Singer dated October 1, 1938, of
all rights of every kind and character in and to all of my acts,
poses, plays and appearances and in and to all recordations of
my voice and all instrumental, musical and other sound effects
produced by me, and in and to all of the results and proceeds
of my services for you, and the right to use my name and like-
ness and reproductions of my voice and sound effects produced
by me in connection with the advertising and exploitation thereof.
I agree that you may use such photographs and recordings in said
photoplay "WIZARD OF OZ" or in any other photoplay or photoplays
and otherwise as you may desire.

All notices served upon Leo Singer in connection with
the aforesaid agreement shall for all purposes be deemed to be
notice to me of the matters contained in such notice.

Very truly yours,

Charles Becker

IHP:em

Each Munchkin under Leo Singer had to sign a stock contract such as this one, signed by
Charley Becker, mayor of Munchkinland. *(Reprinted by permission of Turner Entertainment
Company)*

October 4, 1938

Mr. Leo Singer
c/o Metro-Goldwyn-Mayer Studios
Culver City, California

Dear Mr. Singer:

This will confirm the following agreement amending our agreement
with you dated October 1, 1938, as follows:

 1.   The date "October 3, 1938" appearing in paragraphs 1 and
      2 of said contract is hereby amended to "October 4, 1938".

 2.   Said date of October 4, 1938 is and shall be deemed to be
      the date designated by us for the commencement of your
trip east pursuant to the provisions of said agreement.

 3.   You agree to carry Workmen's Compensation Insurance cover-
      ing all of the midgets employed by you pursuant to said
contract throughout the entire period during which we shall be en-
titled to their services during said period.

 4.   Except as hereinabove expressly provided, said contract
      dated October 1, 1938 is not changed, altered, amended or
affected in any manner or particular whatsoever.

If the foregoing is in accordance with your understanding and agreement, kindly indicate your approval and acceptance thereof in the
space hereinbelow provided.

Very truly yours,

LOEW'S INCORPORATED

By _____
              Vice President

APPROVED AND ACCEPTED:

_____
      (Leo Singer)

In this contract amendment between Loew's Incorporated and Leo Singer, notice that
Singer was to supply workmen's compensation for all the midgets. Eddie Mannix, vice
president, signed for Loew's. *(Reprinted by permission of Turner Entertainment Company)*

came alive, and the register on the counter became filled. "We were so tired, most of us went to bed right away," remembers Jerry Maren, one of the youngest of the bunch.

Each midget who was recruited by Singer signed a contract the next day, promising to work exclusively with Singer—as his employee, not the studio's. The agreement included workmen's compensation, an expenses-paid trip from their homes to Los Angeles and back, and lodgings during their expected stay.

MINIATURE PAYCHECKS, TOO?

Dorothy's dog, Toto, was paid more than the Munchkins. Unfortunately, that's true. For the little cairn terrier, M-G-M cut a weekly check of $125, made out to its owner, Carl Spitz, while trainer Jack Weatherwax worked the dog on the set. Quite an expensive bark.

The highest salaries of the film went to Jack Haley and Ray Bolger: $3,000 each per week. Judy Garland made a mere $500 weekly, while the Munchkins made peanuts. And after Singer took his cut, just the shell was left.

The compensation designated by M-G-M for the Munchkins was $50 a week per midget from November 11, 1938, until the first day of rehearsal, or no later than November 22. After that, Singer was allotted $100 per week for each of the midgets until the expiration of the term. In addition, Singer was contractually obligated to hold the entire group of midgets in Los Angeles for two weeks after completion for possible retakes, added scenes, or changes in the film. If M-G-M needed the services of the midgets for retakes, they would be paid normal weekly wages or prorated wages for work rendered daily, according to the contract. Despite the amounts allotted by M-G-M, Singer had his own plan for how much the midgets would receive.

During the few weeks that Singer crossed the country rounding up midgets through every lead he could grasp, the number just wasn't adding up to the 124 he had promised. He regularly checked in with his agents, such as Thelma Weiss, and

his secretary, Frances Schmeisser, to see if any new little people
had been found. In order to reach the total, he had to strike a
subcontract with the managers of two smaller groups of midgets,
the Harvey and Grace Williams group and the Dolly and Henry
Kramer troupe. Both groups were signed to appear in Los Angeles no later than November 11, which they did. Together, the
little performing troupes brought in fewer then twenty midgets,
but they raised the number close to what was expected of Singer.

An older midget named Major Doyle, who walked with a
cane, thought he could handle the whole deal for M-G-M much
more efficiently than Singer; however, he did *not* receive the
contract, as was reported in accounts over the years. Doyle did
bring a few midgets with him, but they signed a separate contract
with M-G-M, as did several other "independents" near the date
of filming. Manager Fred LaReine brought in four midgets from
New York: Colonel Casper, Howard Marco, Albert Ruddinger,
and George Suchsie. LaReine was one of two or three who by-
passed Singer for a direct contract with M-G-M. Singer knew he
could not magically produce the remainder of the little people,
so he allowed the front office the opportunity of signing walk-
ins and any other independent midgets that M-G-M located.

"Any little person who showed up at the front door of
M-G-M got a job as a Munchkin," says Meinhardt Raabe, who
was awarded the prize role of coroner Munchkin. "I went out
purely on a will-o'-the-wisp. The midget grapevine went around
the country that M-G-M needed little people. On the basis of
that I took a leave of absence from Oscar Mayer Company, where
I worked, and headed out to California."

Raabe signed a contract to be paid by Singer, as did most
of the little people, over whom Singer hovered like a parent over
a newborn. But some of the independents, such as Munchkin
Mickey Carroll, were already under contract to M-G-M at the
time. "My brother Bud did all the talking for me," Carroll says.
"My job had absolutely nothing to do with Singer." Because
Singer had failed to fulfill his original contractual obligation to
supply the complete miniature population for the film, M-G-M
adjusted his payment accordingly. The total number of midgets
was nearly complete. According to some M-G-M records, only

116 midgets worked in the movie; however, documentation has surfaced after much research proving that at least 122 midgets worked in the film, possibly one or two more.

In addition, nearly a dozen children of approximately seven to ten years of age were auditioned and chosen to fill the background of Munchkin City. They were mostly pretty little girls who had some dancing experience, because the number of male midgets was almost double that of the female. The children's finances were handled directly through the front office at M-G-M, and they were paid weekly at the payroll booth, the same as movie extras.

For various reasons, many of the independently signed midgets chose not to associate contractually with Singer and were handled directly by M-G-M's contractual offices. For these performers, the pay scale was the same as that intended for Singer's midgets: $100 a week.

Most of Singer's Munchkins received only half of what was allotted by M-G-M. They were paid $50 per week, and the other half of their allotment went to Singer. Some of the little people who were given lines received a bit more. Jerry Maren, one of the Lollipop Guild, claims he earned $75 a week. But the actors rarely complained about their salaries or fought over who was paid more. Everyone was happy to be working during this, the close of the Depression. In light of the nation's condition, $50 a week was considered a handsome sum. Many of the Munchkins wired much of their income home to help their families; others stashed away their earnings. Moreover, Singer had the right to terminate nearly any of the midgets from the film if he wished, so financial arguments rarely occurred.

It is not known whether Singer discussed these arrangements with the midgets prior to their working on the film. No one recalls. In addition, it would have been out of character for Singer—considered a shrewd businessman—to explain to the midgets that he was pocketing half of their salary each week for his position as their manager. He was not always known to be totally honest.

On the other hand, many of his employees felt he was just. "Singer always treated his people fine; he was a peach," says

Nita Krebs, who was a member of his troupe for many years. "He also bought us things . . . wardrobes, and such." And, according to Munchkin Fern Formica, "He was a money-making man, but he took care of his little people. He was like a father. He was a good man."

TAINTED YELLOW BRICKS

During their six-week stay in Culver City, rumors flew that the midgets were getting involved in odd situations and behaving in a less than civilized manner around town.

Unfortunately, many of the rumors that haunted the Munchkin actors were perpetuated by Judy Garland herself. In 1967, during her third and final guest appearance on "The Jack Paar Show," Garland told the following entertaining story:

PAAR: What about the Munchkins?
GARLAND: They were very tiny.
PAAR: They were little kids?
GARLAND: They were little drunks.
PAAR: Little drunks?
GARLAND: Well, one of them who was about forty asked me for dinner. And I couldn't say I don't want to go: I can't go out with you because you're a midget. I just said, "My mother wouldn't want me to." He said, "Bring your ma, too!"
PAAR: How tall was he?
GARLAND: About two inches high.
PAAR: What could you do with him?
GARLAND: I don't know. They evidently did a lot.
PAAR: There were lots of them.
GARLAND: Oh yeah. Hundreds. Thousands! They put them all in one hotel room—no, not in one room, one hotel. In Culver City. And they all got smashed every night and they picked them up in butterfly nets. They'd slam a tulip in their nose, the poor things. I imagine *they* get residuals.

■■

It was a well-known fact that Garland loved to exaggerate rather than tell the plain truth. Even her daughter Liza Minnelli, in a 1976 CBS "60 Minutes" segment, talked about how Garland felt compelled to stretch stories—even for her personal psychiatrist. (Interestingly, at the time Garland spoke of the little people being drunks with Paar, she was battling an alcohol and drug problem herself. Judy Garland died just two years later, at the age of forty-seven, from what is described by some as an accidental overdose.)

Whatever trouble *did* occur was probably aggravated by the treatment they received from the studio and the public who met them.

M-G-M naturally had interoffice memos that circulated from one executive to another and one technician to another. In some of this correspondence, references to the midgets are less than respectful.

One such memorandum refers to "Mr. Powell—an adult manager—and his two midgets . . ." (implying that the little people weren't adults). Another memo states: "Bus left New York this morning with twenty-eight midgets and two adults." Many of the Munchkins were older than the staff who worked behind the scenes.

Yet another page, referring to a partial list of the little people, notes, "Don't know whether these twelve include any adults, or whether they are all midgets."

Of course, M-G-M was new at employing such a large group of little people; it had never happened before. In one reported incident the studio teacher attempted to round up some of the midgets for school, mistaking them for children. To top that, one of the wardrobe mistresses reportedly attempted to help one shy little "boy" with his costume. "C'mon now . . . I have a little one just like you at home," she told him in a motherly tone. Embarrassed, she realized he was a mature adult when he undressed.

Some of the little actors did not appreciate being treated like children, and they let it be known. Others shook it off.

"In the beginning," remembers Gus Wayne, a Munchkin soldier, "they put us through some rehearsal and talked to us like we were kids. 'Left foot, right foot . . . ' Ya only got two feet! Very difficult," he says sarcastically.

Leo Singer was on the set during much of the filming to make sure that the little people had everything they needed and that their work was running smoothly. "After we got to the studio, they told us that Mr. Singer was in charge of all of the little people," Jerry Maren remembers. "He attended to our eating, and any other activities and such, to take the headache away from M-G-M."

For the most part, recruiting the midgets and making their stay comfortable and their work run smoothly was not too painful for Singer. However, he had confrontations with his midgets, just as the studio expected. One such incident was with gunsling-in' Munchkin Charles Kelley.

"One day in the studio, Kelley came in with guns on his side," remembers little Karl Slover, one of Singer's troupe. "They were real guns. Two of 'em. The director spotted him and told Singer. Singer said, "Oh boy, I better take care of this,' and he found that the guns were real. He told Charley to get out and asked him what the guns were for. Charley said, 'They're for the protection of my wife.' I think Singer threw him out of the movie."

According to many of the Munchkins, Charles Kelley was a jealous midget in the process of divorce from his wife, Jessie, who was also playing a Munchkin in the movie.

Remembers Margaret Pellegrini: "When I got to Hollywood, I was assigned to stay with Jessie Kelley. She had been in show business, and she was like a little mother hen, since she was older. Jessie was a very sweet person.

"On a Sunday morning, I was sitting at the desk writing out Christmas cards, kind of blue and homesick. It was the first time I'd been that far away from home. And I remember this perfectly, like it happened yesterday.

"All of a sudden we get a knock on the door, and here it

Mr. Singer has made a personal request this morning that he be allowed to receive carfare for and send home immediately the following people:

Mr. Kelly - a midget
Mr. Powell - an adult manager - and his two midgets, Gus Wayne and Leo Polinsky.

The reason Mr. Singer gives is that he anticipates a great deal of trouble from these people. He stated that Mr. Kelly tried to kill Mrs. Kelly last night, and that one of Powell's midgets tried to knife his assistant, Mr. Torelli, in an altercation last night.

Pleasant little fellows.

Will you please notify me as to whether or not I should allow them to go?

Keith Weeks.

In a memo from production manager Keith Weeks, the possibility of releasing a few midgets was discussed. However, it is doubtful that any action was taken, because this was the final day of shooting. (Note: "Mr. Powell" refers to Mr. Walter Paul, manager to Munchkins Gus Wayne and Leon Polinsky. According to Wayne, Singer's real problem was that Paul was getting the commission for these midgets.) *(Reprinted by permission of Turner Entertainment Company)* is Jessie's husband, Charley, and he had a knife. He was holding it straight out from his belly. He comes walkin' in. I stepped back. Then I said, 'I'm going outside, I'll leave you two alone.' He says, 'No, you don't,' and shuts the door. I think he said, 'You sit down,' and I started crying and I was shaking. Jessie got him over to the side of the bed and started talking to him, 'cause he had been drinking. Finally he put the knife down and she got him to leave.

"Jessie and I had to move to another hotel because she reported it to Singer and he didn't want us hurt."

Pellegrini and a few of the other little people also remember when Charles Kelley came into the main restaurant one morning during breakfast and grabbed his wife by the hair. "He threw her down and starting rasslin' with her when a few of the little ones grabbed him," Pellegrini says.

In spite of all the rumors of violence among the Munchkins, that was probably the extent of the midgets' mischief. As about any other group, much like participants at a convention, stories get exaggerated. The male midgets seemed to bear the brunt of the gossip. Tall tales about the little men haunted their whole existence in Culver City.

"They had sex orgies in the hotel and we had to have police on just about every floor," said producer Mervyn LeRoy years later.

LeRoy and many of the technicians, as well as others working on the film, found it amusing to go to the studio in the morning and hear the latest about the little people's adventures during their off-hours. The rumor mill seems to operate no matter what size the subjects are—people are people. But probably more stories were told about the little people because it was so unusual to have such a large group of them around.

Escapades of drinking, whoring, and pimping were main topics of conversation. It is doubtful that most of these things actually happened; however, there were a select few who enjoyed an occasional tip o' the bottle. Some enjoyed more tips than others.

"There were two little twins named Mike and Ike [Matina]. God, they were lush-hounds," Karl Slover recalls. "One of them came in the studio drunk one day, and Singer had to send him home."

Munchkin Nels Nelson also remembers the twins. "We used to pit them against each other for laughs," Nelson says. "We'd say, 'Hey, your brother's drinkin' your booze when you're asleep!' and so on. We'd sic them on each other 'cause they argued about their liquor all the time."

Singer wound up getting a call late one evening from the Culver Hotel manager complaining about a few of the little guests being loud and uncontrollable. In no way did it resemble the scenes in Orion Pictures' 1981 movie *Under the Rainbow*, which featured the midgets swinging from chandeliers and trashing the hotel like it was a playground. (Set in 1938 at M-G-M Studios, this motion picture takes a comical peek at the welcoming of more than one hundred midgets to Hollywood for the movie. A subplot of a Nazi midget spy is a feeble attempt at humor. Also, featuring the riotous actions of the midgets "taking over" the hotel they inhabited and running wild in the M-G-M backlot, it all adds up to a terrible movie. The only originals from *The Wizard of Oz* to return to the Yellow Brick Road were Munchkins Jerry Maren and Ruth Robinson Duccini. Agreeably, they felt the movie was awful and an unclear picture of the Munchkins. Although *Under the Rainbow* is intended to be a parody, it furthered rumors about the Munchkins being uncontrollable.)

Nevertheless, there were a few difficulties with some of the little people, as with any group of extras.

"Singer went over to the hotel one night and was still in his nightshirt," Karl Slover recalls. "He walked up the steps and down the hall and he heard someone yelling 'Help!' He got mad. Johnny Pizo also got up and met Singer in the hallway. They looked in the bathroom and here was Charley Ludwig with his face in the toilet bowl, all black and blue. He had fallen in! Singer made Ludwig stay at his house from then on so Mrs. Singer could look after him."

Slover also recalled three related midgets, Charley, Helen, and Stella Royale, drinking excessively, but not causing much trouble in the hotel. "Some of [the Munchkins] raised a lot of cain in the hotel," he says of the whole group.

Other little people preferred to see the city's nightlife. "A group of us girls used to go to a club called the 90-90 Club," remembers Ruth Robinson Duccini. "We loved to go dancing." In the time when vaudeville was still active and theater and night-clubs were booming, the little people crashed the most exclusive of night spots in Los Angeles. Munchkin Murray Wood remembers the midgets packing into a car and going out to a few clubs, where the doormen's eyes would bulge as all the midgets hopped out of the auto.

On the weekends, the Munchkins took to sightseeing and other activities to rest from the studio's grueling hours in front of hot lights. Margaret Pellegrini remembers taking a quick Sunday trip to Tijuana with her roommate Jessie Kelley and reporting to work the next day completely exhausted—but brimming with great memories to write home.

THERE'S NO PLACE LIKE HOLLYWOOD

The first few weeks the Munchkins were at M-G-M, their time was devoted to rehearsals, costume fittings, and more rehearsals.

On a separate soundstage, dance director Bobby Connolly put groups of the actors in lines and showed them a dance step. By their repeat performance, he could gauge which of them were more inclined to dance well and which would simply bob up and down in the background. At this point, the Lullabye League and the Lollipop Guild were chosen. For the Lullabye toe dancers in pink tutus, Nita Krebs, Olga Nardone, and Yvonne Moray were selected. The three little tough guys with an oversized lollipop between them were Jackie Gerlich, Jerry Maren, and Kurt Schneider (a.k.a. Harry Doll).

Other parts for the sequence—including the mayor, coroner, barrister, city fathers, three trumpeters, five Sleepy Heads, twenty-five soldiers, a carriage driver, and five fiddlers—were also cast.

"It was indeed an honor to be chosen out of all of the little people," says Nita Krebs, the Lullabye Leaguer on the left. Krebs also plays one of the four who approach Dorothy near the end of the scene saying, "Follow the Yellow Brick Road."

In the rehearsal hall, there were folding chairs set up, a piano, and a large staircase similar to bleachers in a gymnasium. Here, the Munchkins were each given two mimeographed pages of the scene's songs. They rehearsed the songs until they knew them fairly well. They were not required to memorize the songs perfectly, since the actual Munchkin vocals would be enhanced and dubbed in later. In the same open area, the "Munchkin skip" was taught. This is the same behind-the-foot skip that Dorothy made famous on her trek down the Yellow Brick Road. Most of the Munchkins still remember it.

The staircase was there so the actors playing Munchkins could get accustomed to running up and down it. In the shot after the Munchkins arise, a group of little people quickly scale the steps and wave into the camera as the Sleepy Heads awake from little green eggshells in a huge nest. ("Wake up, you sleepy head,/Rub your eyes,/Get out of bed . . .")

The M-G-M wardrobe department was under tremendous pressure as the deadline for the actual filming drew near. Yards upon yards of multicolored felt were being stitched into oversize—yet tiny—vests, jackets, slippers, bonnets, dresses, and bows. Designer Gilbert Adrian put his personal touch on each and every costume by sketching the rainbow-colored outfits and selecting the exact material in which they would be stitched. One of Hollywood's most creative costume designers, Adrian created oversize buttons, bows, and acccessories to accent the tiny people. Today, some of the actual costumes remain prized pieces in many private collections. Some of the outfits were sold at the M-G-M auction in 1970, and other pieces were reported stolen from the wardrobe department. M-G-M attempted to maintain a tight hold on all wardrobe items through the years, but some pieces did filter out of the studio and into collectors' hands. The mystery of the ruby slippers, several pairs of which mysteriously walked out of the wardrobe department, is still a topic of conversation among fans of the movie. However they came into circulation, the little felt Munchkin pieces, which are delicately stitched, fetch top dollars from Oz aficionados today.

The costumes were only one portion of the Munchkin illusion. Jack Dawn, credited with designing the character makeup, hired nearly twenty extra makeup artists to assist in the creation of Munchkins every morning.

"Makeup was a pain in the ass," says Jerry Maren. "It was cold—freezin'—and you weren't used to getting up that early. It was around five A.M. When we got to the studio, we had to go downstairs in a basement underneath one of the stages. They had about twenty makeup chairs with makeup people ready for us."

The little actors lined up assembly-line fashion for their specially fitted noses, bald-head skin, and assorted hair pieces. One by one, they popped from chair to chair until they were complete. The men required more attention than the women, who rarely wore any type of added hair or extravagant makeup reshaping their facial features. Many of the females donned little flowerpots atop their heads.

"They always put that skullcap on first," remembers Nels Nelson. "Then the hairpiece and the rest. When it got hot in the studio, you'd sweat underneath it and it [the makeup] would run down your face."

Getting the makeup off was another drudgery remembered by a few of the Munchkins. "When we'd take the stuff off, it practically ripped our skin," says Lewis Croft. The spirit gum used in those days was not as sophisticated as the chemicals of today's special-effects makeup. Removing it could sometimes be quite harsh on the skin, as actress Margaret Hamilton always attested, referring to her green pallor as the Wicked Witch of the West.

But once the Munchkins were ready on the set at 8:00

A.M., the work began. For four weeks, Stage 27 came alive from morning to early evening as Munchkins sang and danced and Judy Garland graced their company with her innocent, gleaming eyes and her delicate yet powerful voice.

There may be no more memorable musical moments on film than when the inhabitants of Munchkinland open their mouths to sing. But even now, there is some controversy over whose voices we are actually hearing.

"That is the biggest misconception everybody has," says Munchkin coroner Meinhardt Raabe. "Whenever I wasn't in the action, I was behind the camera watching what was goin' on. All our voices were recorded, and they went through an oscilloscope. For the girls they eliminated the low notes when they rerecorded it so their voices were high. For the boys, they did the opposite. What you hear is actually my voice, but it has been manipulated. There was no dubbing for any part."

According to Raabe, their voices were recorded during the filming by one boom microphone mounted on the huge camera crane. However, this seems unlikely for several reasons.

For the voices to have been recorded during the actual shooting of the scene, several unsolvable problems would have had to have been overcome. For instance, Charley Becker, who played the mayor of Munchkinland, had a thick German accent. The film's mayor speaks perfect English.

In addition, had the Munchkins' voices been recorded during filming, the huge dance sequences would have been a disaster, since the mikes would have picked up the constant rustle and sweep of body movement. Moreover, there would have been no way to recondition the high and low pitches in a recording of men and women singing together. Men and women would have had to have been recorded separately, then the pitches adjusted, and finally the sound mixed. This process could not have been achieved by the relatively primitive audio equipment available in 1938.

It seems obvious that the Munchkins' voices were dubbed in later. In fact, if you observe closely, you can see the worst of the dubbing during the Lollipop Guild's little ditty. Unfortunately, the song and the lip movement hardly come close to matching.

Who then, sang "Ding Dong! The Witch Is Dead"? One of the film's vocal arrangers, Ken Darby, stated emphatically that none of the midgets recorded any of the songs. In the same interview, however, he added, "None of them could carry a tune."

This statement is ludicrous, of course, since many of the midgets successfully sang on Broadway, in other films, and in nightclubs and stage shows for years. Some even made careers out of warbling. In addition, although their differing nationalities, languages, and accents have been thought to have been the reason for dubbing the vocals, only a portion of the group were foreign. Furthermore, an M-G-M daily music report dated December 15, 1938, mentions "an orchestra and three midgets recording scene 2070/Bars 249–265," which seems to indicate at the least that the little people themselves were involved in the dubbing.

A few of the midgets have claimed to have performed in some prerecordings; however, according to many of the surviving midget actors, no *pre*recordings were done for that scene. It was all mixed after filming.

Ken Darby remembers two groups who he says performed the Munchkins' vocals: the King's Men Quartet and the Debutantes. Who actually caroled these film figures to life cannot be verified by any M-G-M documents. Whoever it was, it was a job well done.

The director, Victor Fleming—who later left *The Wizard of Oz* production to direct *Gone with the Wind*—was a competent professional and knew what he wanted. Directing the midgets was a job for which he realized he needed assistance. He had crew members—such as assistant director Al Shoenberg, dance director Bobby Connolly, and production manager Keith Weeks—aid in coordinating the little people and their adherence to schedules. With more than one hundred extras, problems were bound to arise. Upsets in the schedule weren't always caused by the Munchkins, however.

"One time the director yelled at Billie Burke," remembers

Munchkin Gus Wayne. "He really let her have it. She couldn't get over some word or something and, man, he jumped all over her. That had no class. It was right in front of everybody."

Karl Slover remembers a dress rehearsal when the three trumpeters leading the mayor's procession functioned more like the Three Stooges. "We were about the shortest of the bunch. It was little Kayo [Erickson], me, and Major Mite [Clarence C. Howerton]. Every time the director gave the cue for Kayo to come out, he'd stand there like he was asleep. Major Mite and I used to say, 'Come on, Kayo, let's go.' We'd give Kayo a shove and he'd get madder than heck.

"The director had us do it two or three times, and Kayo missed it every time. Finally, the director came over to us and said, 'OK, we can't have this.' So I told him that I could come out on cue, and he said that would be fine. So on film, first comes me, then little Kayo and Major Mite.

"I later heard that Kayo had a sleeping sickness," Slover adds. "He'd get in a fog. Maybe that's why he wouldn't move. He was a nice fellow, though."

The filming was relatively uninterrupted for the Munchkin sequences. Fleming knew exactly how to regroup the little people so that every shot created the illusion of a sea of Munchkins behind the action. Study of the sequences reveals the way he used certain Munchkins—mainly the tinier ones, such as Jeane La-Barbera—in one area of the set after another. LaBarbera pops up all over the place, noticeably out of order regardless of where she is supposed to be stationed in Munchkinland. One second you spot her in a group near the thatch houses; then, in the blink of an eye, she is next to Dorothy. Although their shifting was creatively done, Fleming probably assumed that with the Munchkins' basically matched sizes and rainbow-colored costumes, no one would notice.

The arc lights on the set were intense, both to create the

illusion of being outdoors and to aid the film's embryonic color development. This is one of the earliest successful Technicolor motion pictures. A better vehicle could not have been chosen. The genius of confining the Kansas farm scenes to black and white while the dream is in brilliant color could have easily come from Einstein—it's that inspired—but color technology was still in its infancy, and the set required very bright lighting.

"Because of the huge arc lamps hanging down and creating tremendous heat," says Meinhardt Raabe, "there was a fellow going around the set all the time checking for hot spots with his little meter."

Moreover, the heat made the elaborate lined costumes uncomfortable at times. Some of the Munchkins wore shirts with ruffles, vests, and jackets, as well as several coats of makeup plus hats. "We were almost sweltering," says Raabe, who wore a long, deep blue, layered robe as the coroner.

During breaks in filming, Judy Garland cleared herself a little spot on the steps of the Munchkinland City Hall and chatted with the Munchkins. She was as curious about their lives as they were about her life as a star. "We didn't get much chance to talk to Billie Burke or Margaret Hamilton on the set," says Meinhardt Raabe. "But Judy was just great to us. A very pleasant young girl."

While some of the Munchkins sat Indian style around Garland, sharing a few giggles and some small talk, other little people were busy playing host to visitors on the set.

"Many of the stars at M-G-M would drop by the set and say hello to us Munchkins," remembers Margaret Pellegrini. "We had Mickey Rooney stop by several times. Also Norma Shearer, Eleanor Powell, Myrna Loy, Walter Pidgeon, and Victor McLaglen all stopped by.

"Norma Shearer's kids came with her to the set one day, and we took the kids up the stairs and by the Sleepy Head eggs," says Pellegrini. "They thought that was neat."

Pellegrini saw another famous star at the studio, this one close to her height. "I'm not sure what he was doing at M-G-M, but I saw little Alfalfa from the Little Rascals on a tram at the

studio one morning," she says. "These trams were right outside
the soundstage to take us to other parts of the lot, like the bath-
rooms."

By the time lunch hour rolled around, the Munchkins
were hungry little people. Still in costume, they sometimes were
brought lunches in boxes on the set, or they ate in the studio
commissary. Also, they went across the lot to Marie's Restaurant,
where they usually ate breakfast and dinner. "If you didn't get
there quickly, you'd have to wait in a line that went clear out the
door," remembers Margaret Pellegrini.

The stars retreated to their dressing rooms once break
was called. The lights shut down, and shadows fell on the Yellow
Brick Road. Billie Burke had her nicely decorated tent with its
pink-and-blue interior right alongside the Kansas farmhouse that
fell on the witch. Margaret Hamilton, as she described it, had a
nook in the corner for makeup, but she didn't complain. Judy
Garland had a tent, of sorts, until one day when the studio surprised her—with all the Munchkins watching.

"Near Christmastime, M-G-M presented her with her own
private dressing room with wheels," remembers Margaret Pellegrini. "They had a big red ribbon and bow tied over the door,
and when she came to work a few days before Christmas, she
cut the ribbon. She let us all go inside and look at it."

The holidays for the Munchkins don't seem to have been
very memorable. Only a few recall that December 25. They had
already missed being with their families on Thanksgiving, and
now the most important holiday of the year was approachng and
they were stuck on the Yellow Brick Road waiting for Santa.

"Many of us got homesick," Pellegrini says. "But a lot of
us kept in good touch with our relatives by writing and calling."

Munchkin Ruth Duccini still keeps in her scrapbook the
telegram she received from home during the holiday season. It
was her first Christmas away from family.

"There was a church that had invited a group of us over
to help trim their tree," remembers Alta Stevens. "A bunch of
us went with Grace and Harvey Williams over to the church, and
we all had hot chocolate and sang songs. It was very nice."

Judy Garland wanted to do something very special for the

Munchkins, but what do you get more than 120 little people who have everything? Garland ordered a huge box of candy to be delivered to the set one day and plopped it down on the yellow bricks. She gathered all the little people around. With a "Merry Christmas" and a big smile, she opened the box, inviting all of them to enjoy the expensive chocolates.

"It must have been a twenty-five- or thirty-pound box of chocolates," Margaret Pellegrini says. "It was enormous. That was her Christmas present to us."

And some of the Munchkins remember that at the same gathering Garland went into her dressing room, got her blue fountain pen and a stack of photographs, and signed photos for the little people who had requested a memento from the budding star. She smiled and etched a personalized signature on the studio stills.

These are the treasured few items that remain like relics in the collections of the little people. The autographed photos are yellowed now, but good thoughts always accompany them when the Munchkins glance at the beautiful girl in the portrait, and her autograph underneath.

WINGED MONKEY BUSINESS

For children, the goblinlike Winged Monkeys, servants of the Wicked Witch of the West, are the stuff of nightmares. For the most part, the monkeys were *not* played by the same actors as the Munchkins. Only a few of the more athletic midgets were asked to put on the monkey outfits with battery-powered wings attached to the backs. The wings were motorized, so they would flap while the monkeys were airborne. Harry Monty was one of the actors who played a monkey *and* a Munchkin. Most of those who played the dozen or so brown, flying chimps were too tall to portray Munchkins, Monty says.

Ray Bolger told a story of how the stuntmen were to be paid $25 every time they performed their "swoop" after Dorothy and her companions in the forest.

Victor Fleming assumed payment was $25 for the day. "He kept saying, 'Take 'em up again!' for a retake, and they knew they wouldn't get paid each time," Bolger said. "So they struck the picture. Stopped it cold for a while."

There they were. More than a dozen winged monkeys sitting on chairs with their arms folded and legs crossed arguing with Fleming over money. Finally, the financial arrangement was settled, and back in the air they went, buckled to harnesses that were attached to cables.

The rest of the illusion was created with little rubber monkeys about six inches in height. These molded figurines were suspended from wires in the studio, much as the actor-monkeys were.

The only other Winged Monkeys that M-G-M documents record are actor Sid Dawson, in a wardrobe photograph dated December 13, 1938, and Pat Walshe, the midget stunt double who played Nikko, the head monkey in the witch's castle. Harry Monty rememers another stuntman, named Buster Brody, also playing one of the monkeys.

Meet the Munchkins

3

The Women

Gladys W. Allison
Freda Besky
Josefine Balluck
Christie Buresh
Lida Buresh
Nona Cooper
Elizabeth Coulter
Ethel W. Denis
Hazel I. Derthick (Resmondo)
Jeanette Fern (Fern Formica)
Addie E. Frank
Thaisa L. Gardner
Carolyn E. Granger
Helen M. Hoy
Marguerite A. Hoy
Jessie E. Kelley (Becker)

Emma Koestner
Mitzi Koestner
Dolly Kramer
Nita Krebs
Jeane LaBarbera (Little Jeane)
Hilda Lange
Ann Rice Leslie
Yvonne Moray (Bistany)
Olga C. Nardone (Litttle Olga)
Margaret C. H. Nickloy
Hildred C. Olson
Leona M. Parks
Lillian Porter
Margaret (Margie) Raia
Gertrude H. Rice
Hazel Rice
Ruth L. Robinson (Duccini)
Helen J. Royale (Wojnarski)
Stella A. Royale (Wojnarski)
Elly A. Schneider (a.k.a. Tiny Doll)
Frieda Schneider (a.k.a. Gracie Doll)
Hilda E. Schneider (a.k.a. Daisy Doll)
Elsie R. Shultz
Ruth E. Smith
Alta M. Stevens (Barnes)
Charlotte V. Sullivan
Betty Tanner
Grace G. Williams
Margaret Williams (Pellegrini)
Marie Winters (Maroldo)
Gladys V. Wolff

John Ballas
Franz (Mike) Balluck
John T. Bambury
Charles (Charley) Becker
Henry Boers
Theodore Boers
Eddie Buresh
Mickey Carroll
Colonel Casper
Thomas J. (Tommy) Cottonaro
Lewis Croft (Idaho Lewis)
Frank H. Cucksey
Billy Curtis
Eugene S. David, Jr.
Eulie H. David
Prince Denis
Major Doyle
Carl M. (Kayo) Erickson
Jakob (Jackie) Gerlich
William A. Giblin
Jack Glicken
Joseph Herbst
Jakob Hofbauer
Clarence C. Howerton (Major Mite)
James R. Hulse
Robert Kanter (Lord Roberts)
Charles E. (Charley) Kelley
Frank Kikel
Bernhard (Harry) Klima
Willi Koestner
Karl (Karchy) Kosiczky (Slover)
Adam Edwin Kozicki (Eddie Adams)
Joseph J. Koziel
Emil Kranzler
Johnny Leal
Charles (Charley) Ludwig

Dominick Magro
Carlos Manzo
Howard Marco
Gerard Marenghi (Jerry Maren)
Bela (Ike) Matina
Lajos (Leo) Matina
Matthew (Mike) Matina
Walter Miller
George Ministeri
Harry Monty
Nels P. Nelson
Franklin H. O'Baugh
William H. (W.H.) O'Docharty
Frank Packard
Nicholas Page
Johnny Pizo
Leon Polinsky (Prince Leon)
Meinhardt Raabe
Matthew Raia
Billy Rhodes (Little Billy)
Friedrich (Freddy) Ritter
Sandor Roka
Jimmie Rosen
Charles (Charley) F. Royale (Wojnarski)
Albert Ruddinger
Elmer (Pernell) St. Aubin
Kurt Schneider (a.k.a. Harry Earles, Harry Doll)
Charles Silvern
Garland (Earl) Slatten
Elmer Spangler
Carl Stephan
George Suchsie
August Clarence Swensen
Arnold Vierling
Gus Wayne
Victor Wetter
Harvey B. Williams

Johnny Winters (Maroldo)
Murray Wood

The Children (those names available)

Betty Ann Cain (Bruno)
Joan Kenmore
Shirley Ann Kennedy
Priscilla Montgomery
Valerie Shepard
Viola White (Banks)

"WE WELCOME YOU TO . . ."

It may have seemed like a cast of a thousand, however, it was a mere 124 or so. That is the number Leo Singer was contracted to supply M-G-M. Of the consistently reported 124 Munchkins, only 31 survivors (this includes three of the children) could be located around the United States for interviews. Based on the dockets that have turned up in private Oz collections (such as an incomplete daily sign-in sheet) plus M-G-M legal records and extensive research, I have compiled a list of the names of 122 of the midgets. It is doubtful that any more than one or two additional midgets were in the cast. Nearly a dozen children are reported to have played Munchkins, so the total number of individuals hired to play Munchkins seems to have been about 134 (midgets plus children). Therefore, this is probably the first and only definitive Munchkin cast list.

After half a century, it is natural that the Munchkins' whereabouts were hard to trace; I have gone to great lengths to include only those who actually participated in the motion picture. (Several little people approached me during my research claiming to be ex-Munchkins when in fact they were not.)

This *is* the most complete answer ever compiled to the often asked question "What ever happened to the Munchkins?" As you will see, most of the little people who lived in Munchkinland have led an Oz-some past.

Jerry Maren was just eighteen when he got the telegram from Loew's Incorporated that requested his presence in Oz. It guaranteed six weeks' work, transportation, food, "the works," he says.

Born on January 24, 1920, Maren was really named Gerard Marenghi. He took dancing lessons when he was young and aspired to be an actor. In November 1938, standing just three foot four, he met up with the Oz-bound group of little people in New York and went by bus to California. There he was chosen to be the Munchkin who hands Dorothy a welcoming lollipop.

"I remember they had a monstrous crew on the set," Jerry says. "A man who wore tall boots would go into the pond and fix the lilies and then walk out, and other crew members would mop up the water. When we had time, we used to sneak off and try to watch the other movies being made. We ran into everybody. I snuck over to watch *Lady of the Tropics* with Hedy Lamarr."

The Wizard of Oz was the first of many movies Jerry made. After *Oz*, he went directly into a few Our Gang comedies, and he also had a role in *At the Circus*, starring the Marx Brothers.

Some time after that, Jerry underwent brief hormonal treatments to increase his height. "I started dreaming how great sports and things would be for me if I were taller," he says. But he grew only a few inches, and after waking up in the morning with aching limbs, he decided to discontinue the injections. So Jerry remained a little person, and he is now quite well satisfied with his stature.

He played Buster Brown on television and radio during

ABOVE: The film *Under the Rainbow*, 1981, starring Chevy Chase, re-created the "making" of the Munchkin scene and relied heavily on rumors that the midgets wreaked havoc in their hotels. The unsuccessful film used mostly dwarfs instead of midgets. *(Courtesy of Orion Pictures)* LEFT: Here, on one of the final days of shooting, some of the little people pose for one last photograph together before they depart for their many destinations. *(Courtesy of Beverly Smith)*

ABOVE: The filming of Munchkinland was one of the most elaborate undertakings in moviemaking history. *(Copyright 1939 Loew's, Inc., renewed © 1966 by M-G-M)* OPPOSITE TOP: Producer Mervyn LeRoy (just left of Judy Garland) and director Victor Fleming (holding Toto) congratulate the Munchkins on a scene well done during one of the last days of production in December 1938. *(Courtesy of Doug McClelland, copyright 1939 Loew's, Inc., renewed © 1966 by M-G-M)* RIGHT: Judy Garland signed a photograph for Munchkin Mickey Carroll's twin sister, who really spells her name Jennie and is of average size. *(Courtesy of Mickey Carroll)*

OPPOSITE: Munchkin Hazel Derthick Resmondo, visiting Marilyn Monroe on the set of *Bus Stop*. *(Courtesy of Hazel Resmondo)* ABOVE RIGHT: Actress Myrna Loy visits the set and meets the tiniest of all the Munchkins, Olga Nardone. *(Courtesy of Victor Wetter)* RIGHT: Actress Margaret Hamilton signed this photograph to Munchkin Hazel Derthick Resmondo on the set. *(Courtesy of Mark Collins)*

LEFT: Actress Billie Burke and actor Ed Wynn in 1957. Burke accepted the role of Glinda the Good Witch but Wynn had declined the offer to play the Wizard. BELOW LEFT: Actor Victor McLaglen visits M-G-M's Lot 2 and poses with some of the little people. Left to right: Billy Curtis, John Ballas, Daisy Doll, McLaglen, Charles Silvern (top), Gracie Doll, Alta Stevens, Robert Kanter, and Dominick Magro. *(Courtesy of Anna Mitchell)* OPPOSITE TOP: The Pasadena Tournament of Roses Parade in January 1939 featured a float promoting *The Wizard of Oz*. Several Munchkins, including the mayor, Charley Becker, and the trumpeter Karl Slover, were featured on the float, which was a joint effort of M-G-M and Culver City. *(Courtesy of the Academy of Motion Picture Arts and Sciences)* OPPOSITE BOTTOM: At the premiere of the movie, Tuesday, August 15, 1939, several of the Munchkins still residing in California were asked by M-G-M to don the colorful costumes at Grauman's Chinese Theatre. Left to right: Nona Cooper, Victor Wetter, Tommy Cottonaro, Billy Curtis, and Jerry Maren as the mayor. *(Courtesy of Allen Lawson)*

LEFT: Premiere Night: In the mayor's costume, Jerry Maren greets Chico Marx at Grauman's Chinese Theatre. Maren had recently finished a Marx Brothers movie, *At the Circus. (Courtesy of the Academy of Motion Picture Arts and Sciences)* BELOW LEFT: One of the children who played Munchkins, Priscilla Montgomery (left) poses with friend Margaret Pellegrini, also a Munchkin and in her teens. *(Courtesy of Margaret Pellegrini)* BELOW CENTER: Little Karchy (Karl Slover) and Margaret Pellegrini, two Munchkins who were once sweethearts. *(Courtesy of Margaret Pellegrini)* BELOW RIGHT: "Lil' Alabam" (Margaret Pellegrini), the Munchkin with the fantastic memory, in 1988. *(Courtesy of Margaret Pellegrini)*

ABOVE LEFT: Mickey Carroll holds his nose at Stella Royale's smelly fur stole. Idaho Lewis Croft is doing the romancing in this snapshot, taken outside the M-G-M lot. *(Courtesy of Ruth Robinson Duccini)* ABOVE CENTER: Mickey Carroll accepts an autographed poster from President Harry Truman while serving as master of ceremonies for a celebration in Truman's home state, Missouri, October 7, 1945. *(Courtesy of Mickey Carroll)* RIGHT: Mickey Carroll as he appeared in the 1930s, when he performed in nightclubs. Still in his teens here, Carroll was listed as the fastest tap dancer in the world by *Ripley's Believe It or Not*. *(Courtesy of Mickey Carroll)* BELOW: Mickey Carroll was presented a home-run bat by one of the St. Louis Cardinals. Carroll can be spotted most seasons at Busch Stadium rooting for his favorite team and signing autographs (1988). *(Courtesy of Mickey Carroll)* BELOW RIGHT: Also called the Wizard of Oz, baseball hero Ozzie Smith of the St. Louis Cardinals poses with his buddy, Munchkin Mickey Carroll. *(Photo by Stephen Cox)*

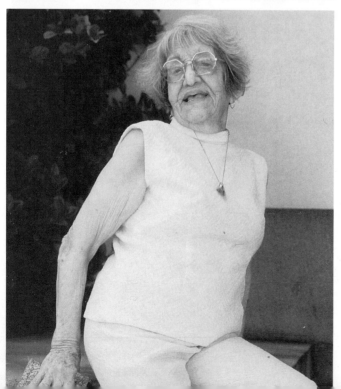

TOP LEFT: Hazel Derthick Resmondo worked as young Jerry Mathers' stand-in for "Leave It to Beaver" during the 1950s. Mathers grew, but she didn't, so the studio fitted her with lifts. *(Courtesy of Hazel Resmondo)* CENTER LEFT: Several years after *Oz*, friends (left to right) Buster Resmondo, Jessie Kelley Becker, Hazel Derthick Resmondo, and Charley Becker got together. Buster and Hazel were married, as were Charley and Jessie. *(Courtesy of Hazel Resmondo)* LEFT: Hazel Derthick Resmondo, a resident of the Eastern Star Home in Los Angeles, still loves to talk about *Oz* (1988). *(Photo by Stephen Cox)* ABOVE: W. H. O'Docharty, who played the little man on the back of Dorothy's horse-drawn coach, as he appears today at his home in Texas. *(Courtesy of Lillian O'Docharty)*

LEFT: Nels Nelson (left) and Jerry Maren, who met in Oz, are still friends and play golf together. *(Photo by Stephen Cox)* ABOVE: Munchkin Jerry Maren as the original Buster Brown for television. *(Courtesy of Jerry Maren)* BELOW: Jerry Maren points to a painting of his most famous role, the middle Munchkin, who hands Dorothy the lollipop. Today he is semiretired and living in California. *(Photo by Stephen Cox)*

Famous fighter Primo Carnera puts his dukes up for this gag shot with "the wrestling midgets" (left to right): Harry Monty, Billy Curtis, and Jerry Maren. *(Courtesy of Harry Monty)*

RIGHT: Little "Johnnie," Gus Wayne, comes up short next to a skid load of cigarette paper for the Philip Morris Company in this promotional photo (January 25, 1949). *(Courtesy of Gus Wayne)* BELOW: Munchkin Gus Wayne and his wife, Olive Brasno, in their Florida home, 1988. Brasno turned down the role of a Munchkin because she was making more money on the road. *(Photo by Stephen Cox)*

ABOVE: The original "Little Oscar," Meinhardt Raabe, with the famous Oscar Mayer Wienermobile, which still tours the country in promotions. *(Courtesy of Meinhardt Raabe)* LEFT: Munchkin coroner Meinhardt Raabe in 1988. *(Courtesy of Jean Nelson)*

Silent-film star Harold Lloyd smiles for the camera with the Doll family siblings who portrayed Munchkins. Left to right: Tiny, Harry, Daisy, and Gracie Doll. *(Courtesy of Margaret Pellegrini)*

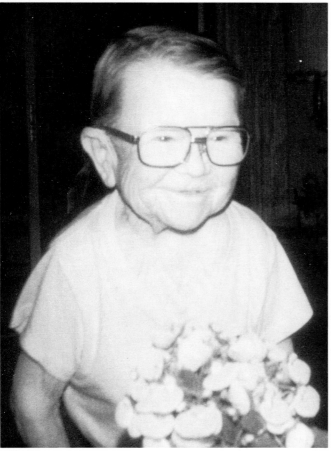

ABOVE: The Doll family in 1956. Left to right: Daisy, Tiny, Gracie, and Harry. *(Courtesy of Tiny Doll)* LEFT: Lollipop Guild member Harry Doll, one month before his death in 1984. *(Courtesy of Anna Mitchell)*

the 1950s and 1960s and has been doing McDonald's commercials under the heavy costume of Mayor McCheese or the Hamburglar for several years. He is constantly recognized as the little guy in the black tuxedo who scatters confetti at the end of each "Gong Show." Maren's list of television appearances is as long as that of any Hollywood star.

Jerry and his wife, Elizabeth, also an actress and a little person, live near Los Angeles; their home is completely designed for little people, with lowered counters and smaller chairs, tables, and couch. As he chews his ever present stogie, which is almost bigger than he is, and leans back glancing outside at his pool, Jerry seems to enjoy his retirement and talking about his most famous role, as one of the Lollipop Guild. His golf game is good, he says, and he plays softball as well. Although he and Elizabeth are semiretired, Jerry is still one of the "biggest" midget actors in Hollywood.

Fern Formica, who was also known as Johnnie Fern McDill and then renamed Jeanette Fern by Leo Singer, sang à la Mae West as Diamond Lil when she was just a tot. "Mae West called me her miniature double," Fern says.

Fern joined Singer's Midgets shortly before *The Wizard of Oz* at the request of Singer, who spotted her talent for entertaining. She worked as one of his troupe in the Midget Village at the San Diego World's Fair, then costarred in *The Terror of Tiny Town* with forty other midgets.

Born on January 17, 1925, "at ten-thirty in the morning on a Saturday," she says M-G-M didn't know she was only thirteen years old when she acted as what she calls a "Munchkin Maid." She was cast as a Munchkin while working with Singer, and she stayed at his home while making the movie. "The film was like a wonderland," she remembers. This role was the beginning of a good career, although that was not how she thought of it at the time.

"Career? Who knew what a career was? It was work. We

were just trying to live!" Fern says. Looking back at her life, she is quite proud of the movie, and also of her one son and her grandchildren, for whom she collects Oz mementos.

She's now sixty-three and skillfully balances a cigarette out of the side of her mouth while talking. Living in Hemet, California, Fern owns and runs a ceramic shop and expertly teaches all aspects of the craft part-time. Her newest pet project is her little Munchkin Maid music boxes. And the ceramic pieces are certifiably Munchkin-made.

Fern adds: "When Judy Garland was on this talk show years later, she said a grievous thing about the Munchkins. She said, 'Oh, those freaky little things.' I thought, my God, what has happened to Judy? The little people never harassed her. They didn't let us get that close to her. We were well mannered and knew not to crowd the star. It was her own physical and mental condition that made her come out with a thing like that. How sad, but a lot of things in life are sad."

In the opening of the Munchkin scene, when the Munchkins come out, you'll notice a little fellow emerging from a manhole. Don't blink. Just then **Mickey Carroll** saunters right across the screen, big—or small—as life, in a deep purple cloak with a yellow flower sticking out of his striped vest. He also plays one of the fiddlers who escorts Dorothy out of the land of Oz (second from left). "I did voice-overs for several of the Munchkins," Mickey says.

Now, at age sixty-nine, Mickey reflects with much pride on his entertainment career. His pictures of Judy Garland and other celebrities he's worked with or met hang on the wall of his office. Mickey started tap dancing and performing when he was in grade school, and he became a one-man act that traveled around to nightclubs and theaters. He was closely managed by his older brother, Bud.

His fondest memories of being on the road include dancing with Donald O'Connor and his sisters, and having Ronald Reagan room with him briefly in Hollywood while visiting relatives stayed in young Reagan's apartment.

But his trip to the M-G-M studio is not one of Mickey's fondest memories. "Bud and I were on our way out to make *The Wizard of Oz* when we had a big accident in Albuquerque. A truck hit us head-on. We had to stay there for weeks. We sued the company and won."

Mickey arrived late on the set and missed almost all the rehearsals, but M-G-M put him under contract with thoughts of using him in more motion pictures. He lived in Judy Garland's home while making the movie, he says. "We were friends when she was in theater. She called me and asked me to come out to make the movie. I said, 'What the hell is *The Wizard of Oz?*' "

Mickey's real name is Michael Finocchiaro; he has a twin sister, Jennie, who stands five foot four, and another sister, Mary, and brother, Leo, of average height. Born in St. Louis, Mickey returned to the Gateway to the West after his nearly ten-year stint on the road and has lived there ever since.

He still owns and runs Standard Monument Company, a job that was passed down from his stepfather many years ago. "After I got out of show business, I came home and worked in the shop and eventually took that over," he says.

In more recent years, Mickey has given much of his time to promote *The Wizard of Oz* and his role as a Munchkin while affiliating the appearances he makes with charities. His pet projects are raising money for the Special Olympics and other needy causes. The plaques on his office wall commend him for many hours of fund-raising for such causes as the USO, the Muscular Dystrophy Association, the Children's Miracle Network, the Ronald McDonald Houses, and countless others.

When asked what he remembers most about the Oz movie, Mickey says, "Probably how beautiful Judy was. And her voice. She was fantastic. And how she used to get tired on the set. . . . When we sang the songs on the set, some of us Munchkins used to joke and say, 'Ding dong, the witch is dead, which old witch, the son of a bitch!' I also remember how the pond leaked and we'd slip on the Yellow Brick Road sometimes. They'd have some guy come out and mop it up."

Mickey picks up a piece of mail from a stack and shows it to his sister. It is addressed "Mickey Carroll, Munchkin. St. Louis, Mo." He is surprised it reached him. "I get all kinds of fan mail," Mickey says.

When you step inside **Nita Krebs's** house, you can guess which Munchkin she played from the mementos of dancers on her shelves and a large painting of a pink ballerina hanging prominently. Nita played the member of the Lullabye League on the left. She was also the woman who darts out and says "Follow the Yellow Brick Road" as Dorothy prepares to leave.

Nita, who was trained in ballet when she was young, entered the United States with Leo Singer. She was born in Czechoslovakia, "which was then Sudetenland and now it is Czechoslovakia again," she explains in her high-pitched, tiny voice with a tilt of her head.

Nita is eighty-two now; she retired to Florida in the 1950s after a long life of performing in vaudeville and stage shows with Singer's Midgets. After *Oz* she did not grow any; she has remained three foot eight, a height that did not inhibit her work at all. She also starred opposite Little Billy Rhodes as the gang moll in *The Terror of Tiny Town* and sang a solo in that film. "Dancing came easy to me," she admits with a noticeable accent. "And I tell you one thing . . . the memories are wonderful. Since my childhood, I've had a wonderful life."

She still remembers a particular day on the set of *Oz*. "I remember this so well. I'll never forget this. . . . There was this little body of water, a pond. And I was tired, I suppose. I was sitting down, and the costumes we had were long, and my costume dipped right into the water. They were ready to shoot the scene. We always had ladies around to help with costumes, and one came over. Whatever was wet, she chopped it off. She snipped it right off!"

Margaret (Williams) Pellegrini was also known as Popcorn and Lil' Alabam to her friends and colleagues. She was a little Southern gal who got whisked away from her hometown of Sheffield, Alabama, to a movie set to be a Munchkin. It's the kind of dream come true that movies are made of.

Margaret, who is sixty-five, was born around the corner from where Helen Keller lived, on September 23, 1923. "I got a letter from Thelma Weiss in Hollywood to come out to make the movie," Margaret says. "My height then was three foot five, but I've grown since. Now I'm about four feet tall."

If you look closely, you can spot Margaret in several corners of Munchkinland—even as one of the Sleepy Heads. M-G-M used her in more than one place because she was so small, perfect for the setting. And she still knows the entire scene by heart. It was a dream to make the movie, and she has never regretted it, remembering almost every detail as though it were yesterday.

"For us girls, our dresses were so big and we had such big petticoats, that we had some ladies who were there to help us go to the bathroom," Margaret remembers shyly. "We'd go to sit on the commode and we couldn't lift 'em up enough. The ladies had to help us lift 'em. It seemed odd havin' someone help you go potty at our age."

With a bit of a raspy voice, Margaret looks back on *Oz* as "a fantastic experience." Afterward, she traveled with some midget troupes and later married an average-size man, ex-fighter Willie Pellegrini. They had two children, Margaret Jo and William Joseph, Jr. (Just recently, she became a great-grand-Munchkin.) After her marriage in 1943, she devoted her life to raising her children and steered clear of show business, except for a movie in which she appeared in 1971, *Johnny Got His Gun*.

Today Margaret is widowed and makes Glendale, Arizona, her home. She has appeared frequently at the Oz festivals in Chesterton, Indiana, and Liberal, Kansas, and welcomes invitations to reminisce about her favorite movie. Her memory for names, places, dates, and times is fantastic. She saved much from her show business and traveling days and is planning to devote one room in her house to her Oz collectibles.

Karl (Karchy) Slover says he was the tiniest of the male Munchkins. "I couldn't even reach the doorknob," he says. He's grown now, from three feet tall when he played a trumpeter in *The Wizard of Oz* to four foot four. His father was six foot six. "Mr. Singer told me I would grow," Karl says. "He seemed to know who would and who wouldn't grow later in life."

Originally, Karl's last name was Kosiczky. Born in Hungary, he changed his name to Slover when he became a U.S. citizen in 1943. His nickname, Karchy, originated when he was working with Singer's Midgets and there were too many midgets named Karl. "Karchy," which is Hungarian for Karl, was pinned on him.

Karchy played the first of the three trumpeters who lead the mayor's procession. He also donned a cute pink outfit as one of the little Sleepy Heads rising from the huge egg. Besides *Oz*, he worked in a two-reeler with Laurel and Hardy, a Ritz Brothers film, and a movie with Alice Faye. He played the barber and the bass player in *The Terror of Tiny Town*, and you can also spot him in the baby carriage in *The Lost Weekend*, a 1945 blockbuster starring Ray Milland.

For many years Karchy performed with Singer's group all over the country. He had chubby little cheeks, a wide grin, and a Hungarian accent. "We knew English when we did *The Wizard of Oz*," Karchy clarifies. "I've read in places that all the Munchkins were German and they didn't know how to speak English. We learned way before that."

Karchy remembers the first day on the set of *Oz*: "They took us through the studio. Here they had these fruit trees. Well, at the time, I didn't know they were rubber. They looked very real. I saw the trees move, and I said, 'What the heck?' My roommate thought I was nuts, and we kept walking around, and then he saw it too. About that time, the propman said, 'Oh, there's a man in each tree.' That tickled me."

Today, Karchy, who is sixty-nine, remains basically retired and lives with a family he has known for many years in Tampa, Florida. He trains little poodles, which perform at various functions, and he also keeps up with other activities around his house, such as mowing the lawn and gardening.

Dolly Kramer was once labeled "Queen of the Midgets" and "America's Tiniest Bombshell of Song."

Now at age "seventy plus," as she says, Dolly lives in Miami Beach and loves the climate there. She's four feet tall and has grown just a few inches since *Oz*—in which she played a Munchkin villager.

"Singer contacted our group," Dolly says of the troupe she and her husband, Henry, headed. "We went out to California to do the movie. Since Singer had the contract with M-G-M, we had made a special deal with him."

Of the filming, she says, "I remember that it was an especially cold November in California that year. As soon as we had to do a scene, the lights went up. In the morning, the lights went up and made us warm. We wanted that in the morning."

Dolly and Henry married when she was sixteen and he was eighteen. She changed her real name, Henny, to Dolly since "Henny" sounded too much like her husband's name. Henry, an average-size adult, managed a group of performing midgets with Dolly as the lead singer and dancer. They traveled across the United States playing many nightclubs and show houses when vaudeville was strong.

Now retired, Dolly has lived in a high-rise apartment for many years. Her husband died in 1981, but she keeps busy with a women's club at her apartment complex. "I can't entertain anymore because of my health, but I'm doing OK," she says.

Gus Wayne says he didn't grow any taller after *Oz*, "I just got heavier." At the height of four foot four, this Munchkin soldier was a lad of eighteen when he left New Jersey with his pal Leon Polinsky to make *The Wizard of Oz*. "I was very young at the time, and the money sounded good. So I was gone. I had a ball."

Today, Gus resembles a miniature Jackie Gleason, with a sauve style to match. He and his wife of twenty-seven years, Olive

Brasno, also a little actress, have lived in Florida for nearly fifteen years. Gus and Olive argue with the bite and humor of Ralph and Alice Kramden on "The Honeymooners."

Olive, who isn't quite the height of Gus, says she was offered the role of a Munchkin as well but declined. "They offered me seventy-five dollars a week, and in vaudeville we were making a hundred and fifty."

For Wayne, *Oz* was just a portion of a career filled with media work. He worked as the Baker for Sunshine Biscuit Company for a few years and also boxed at the Steel Pier, alongside other acts like Abbott and Costello and the Three Stooges. For seven years he put on the bellhop uniform and shouted "Call for Philip Morris." This catchphrase became famous, as did the little bellhops who delivered the line on radio and television and in personal appearances around the country. Because of its popularity, Gus was only one of several Little Johnnies hired and trained to tour for the famous promotion.

Gus then moved on to Piper Aircraft, where he was a small parts mechanic until he retired in the 1970s in Florida with his wife.

He says, "When we were making the movie, I thought for sure it was gonna be a hit. Especially the songs; they were out of this world. Truthfully, would you believe, I haven't seen the whole picture?"

Meinhardt Raabe (pronounced "mine-heart rob-by") was probably the most educated of the small actors. This may have been why he was given the role of the Munchkin coroner, who pronounces the Wicked Witch dead and unscrolls a huge certificate of death. Born on September 2, 1915, in Wisconsin (his parents were German), he stands four foot eight now; he's grown six inches since he was twenty.

Meinhardt earned his bachelor of arts degree in accounting from the University of Wisconsin and his master of arts in business administration from Northwestern University, all the while juggling a career—of sorts, anyway—in show business. "Years ago, the public conception was small body, small mind," he says. "The door was slammed shut in my face as far as an accounting career.

"There was a well-established midget grapevine around the country," Meinhardt says. "So I went to California when I heard M-G-M needed little people."

Meinhardt had already worked in midget shows at the Chicago World's Fair in 1934, the San Diego World's Fair in 1935, and the Texas Centennial of 1936. His work in *Oz*, however, is his most memorable.

"The casting director picked me as a result of my public-speaking experience, I assume," Meinhardt says. "I probably had a little bit better diction and enunciation than maybe some who were foreign born.

"I went around and got autographs of all the people associated with the picture," he says. "Judy wrote 'To Meinhardt, a perfect coroner and a perfect person too. Love from Judy' on a picture I still have in my scrapbook. I also have Jack Dawn, the makeup man, and Mr. Brown, the chief electrician, along with Margaret Hamilton and Billie Burke, Ray Bolger, Jack Haley, and Bert Lahr. It was fun."

Before and after *Oz*, Meinhardt worked for the Oscar Mayer Company as their mascot, Little Oscar, touring in promotions for the company and its meat line. After the market widened, he took on four protégés as Oscar, Jrs. It was during this time that he met his wife, Marie, also a little person.

In more recent years, Meinhardt worked in the public school system in Pennsylvania as a special education teacher, also instructing in horticulture. He now lives in a retirement community owned by the J. C. Penney Company in Florida, where he continues to teach horticulture but is basically retired. The Raabes travel frequently.

Hazel (Derthick) Resmondo can't hear very well anymore, but she can talk plenty. "I'm from Oklahoma. Okies love to talk," she explains.

She's nearing her mid-eighties now, stands a whopping four foot four ("I was one of the bigger ones," she says, remembering her *Oz* days), and can still proudly do the splits and stretch like an Olympic hopeful. It's a carryover from her days as a young toe dancer.

If you look closely, you can see a lone Munchkin villager who is waving ferociously as the Munchkins pour out of their village huts. "The director said wave, so I did," she says. "Everyone else stopped, but I guess I didn't."

Her hearing and eyesight have slipped a bit over the years, but she keeps busy with her correspondence and friends at the Eastern Star Home in Los Angeles, where she now resides. She's packed show business mementos from her career in all corners of her room. Her photo album includes shots of her and Jerry "The Beav" Mathers from her nearly five-year stint as his stand-in on TV's "Leave It to Beaver." And, of course, she has prominent photographs of her late husband, Joe (Buster) Resmondo, whom she still adores. Buster was also a little person, but not an *Oz* cast member.

Hazel loves to talk about *The Wizard of Oz*, and if you ask, she'll do her "Munchkin laugh," gladly. But she doesn't laugh when she remembers her Munchkinlike salary: "Singer hardly paid me anything. There wasn't any union or guild or anything for us then. When I complained, he said, 'If you don't like your job, you can go home.' I stayed, but I didn't know how to stand up for myself like I can now."

Ruth (Robinson) Duccini met her husband, Fred, also a little person, in the restaurant where the Munchkins regularly dined. Fred was just another face among the little people at the eatery, but he had a good job at a nearby hotel and chose not to act in the movie. "We used to call the restaurant Ptomaine Marie's."

Ruth laughs. She has a pleasant smile and very fond memories of *Oz*.

For Ruth, being a Munchkin introduced her not only to her husband but also to one of her closest friends, Alta Stevens, who was a Munchkin as well. Ruth had been with the Harvey Williams group, performing in stage shows and carnivals around the country. *Oz* was her first movie, and oddly enough her last film was a cameo appearance in *Under the Rainbow*—as a Munchkin.

"In *Under the Rainbow* I got into trouble," she says. "They had a lot of little people out there playing Munchkins who never worked in a picture before. Chevy Chase got up and said something really rude to them, and I complained about it later. The producers didn't like that, but I didn't care. I got my paycheck. That's why no one heard much about me in the movie's publicity. Jerry Maren and I were the only little people from the original *Wizard of Oz* to appear in the film."

After marrying, Ruth had two children of normal height, and she now has grandchildren to watch grow. Though retired, she tries to stay very active. She and Freddy live near Laughlin, Nevada, and bear the extreme heat during the summer.

"There's something I'm most proud of, though," she points out. "I worked as a riveter on the inner wing of the C-54 transports used in the war. I could get in spots where others couldn't."

Nels Nelson remembers how he got the role of a Munchkin: "A man called me and insisted on taking me down there to M-G-M. How he got my number, I'll never know. I lived in the valley here."

Nels has remained in California. He was born on November 24, 1921, and passed his seventeenth birthday in a rehearsal hall singing "Ding Dong! The Witch Is Dead" with a hundred other midgets. Not a traditional celebration, but he was having fun.

Sometimes, Nels remembers, the fun was at the expense of one of the Munchkins. "There was this one little guy. He wasn't too bright. He wanted a cigar real bad, so they sent him over to a false-fronted cigar store on the back lot. He stood there and stood there. He didn't understand. I think they had to go get him, but we got a laugh out of it."

Nels also says, "I think the remarkable thing about those days is that our meals were thirty-five cents for lunch. Good lunches." Prices may have risen, but, oddly enough, Nels's height has done the opposite. "I was about four foot six then and now I'm about four foot three. I shrunk!"

His height doesn't affect his golf game, though, and he enjoys staying active. He's in his second marriage, and he and his wife, Gloria, have two children.

After *Oz*, Nels went into real estate with his brother but still worked occasionally in show business. The longest he's stayed in any part was twelve years as a stand-in for the kids on the "Lassie" TV series. Once he was injured in an episode of "Bonanza" called "Hoss and the Leprechauns." It happened when he was hoisting another little person onto his shoulders for a scene. "Just then I felt my hip shift," he says. That was it for his acting and stunts, and he decided to call it quits in show biz.

Harry Monty is eighty-four, but you'd never know it. He's very trim, still well-built, and he exercises regularly. Harry stopped lifting weights several years ago, but in his younger years a larger person would have thought twice before tangling with him.

Born in Russia, Harry came with his parents to the United States when he was very young. He stands four feet five and a half inches now, about the same as he did when he played a Munchkin soldier and a Winged Monkey in the Wicked Witch's army of villains.

"For the Winged Monkeys, they put a harness on us and we swooped down to the ground, one after another," he says. "I remember one of the other monkeys was Buster Brody, but most of the others were a bit taller than me. They weren't really small midgets. . . . This scene only took about a day to film."

He doesn't remember having any fear of his cable breaking when the monkeys were suspended in air, but, after all, he was on his way to becoming one of Hollywood's best midget stuntmen.

After *Oz*, Harry went directly into another film, doubling for Johnny Sheffield in *Tarzan Finds a Son*. He later landed stunt and doubling jobs in some of Hollywood's finest, including *The Court Jester*, *Papillon*, *How the West Was Won*, and *Hello, Dolly!* His television credits include episodes of "Bonanza," "Bewitched," "Daniel Boone," "Lost in Space," and a string of commercials. He now lives in Hollywood.

"I'm basically retired now, but if something good comes along, I might take it," Harry says.

Jeane LaBarbera was always—and still is—known as Little Jeane. She was just over twenty-four inches tall when she played a Munchkin villager in *Oz*, she says. Now she's about three feet tall and has one of the cutest faces you've ever seen. Her voice is tiny yet pleasing.

Handled by the William Morris Agency, Little Jeane "inched her way to the top" as she says, when it came to theater. Her appearances have included the London Palladium, the Hippodrome in New York, and several Broadway productions. Her scrapbook of clippings and photographs is enormous.

She and her husband, Robert Drake, were known as the Comedy Cut-Ups when they performed one of the most unique husband-and-wife acts together. He was six feet tall and she all of two. They are approaching their forty-fifth wedding anniversary. "Ouch," she says, referring to her age.

Born in Italy, Jeane received her schooling and grew up on Long Island. She was a concert violinist with her own custom-fitted instrument when she was discovered by an agent. That encounter led to a long, prosperous career. Interestingly, Little Jeane played opposite another *Wizard of Oz* alumnus, Bert Lahr, in a vaudeville sketch titled "Beach Babies," written by Jeane. It was so successful that they toured together for several years.

The Drakes are now retired at their large Florida home, with years of show business memories, including Jeane's of *Oz*.

52

Murray Wood was born on June 12, 1908, in Nova Scotia and started his career in show business by singing with Kate Smith onstage in New York. "I never took a step back in my career," Murray boasts. "I was successful all the way."

He only stands four foot two, about the same height he was when he married Jean Lanier, also a performer, but of normal height.

Murray played a soldier in the Munchkin army and has mostly fond memories of *Oz*. "It was a fantasy, and I always thought the film would do well. From the start." Nevertheless, trying to collect his paycheck was not such a fantasy.

"On the last day of shooting, I went looking for Leo Singer for my paycheck, and I couldn't find him anywhere. Someone said he was up the street, and I went running after him. He was going away from the studio when I got to him. I'm not sure whether I would've gotten paid if I hadn't run after him."

Wood had been a nightclub and stage singer and a superior master of ceremonies since he was young, playing New York's Irish Village and many other stops around the country. He was also a member of Nate Eagle's Hollywood Midgets troupe, who entertained vaudeville audiences. Later, when he and Jean moved to Florida, he worked in the TV series "Gentle Ben" for two years as a stand-in and bit actor. The couple have lived in Florida ever since.

The four Doll siblings are special not only because of their involvement in *The Wizard of Oz*—all as Munchkins—but also because of the unusual phenomenon of four little people in one family.

"There were seven kids total," says **Tiny Doll**, the only survivor of the four who played Munchkins. "I have one brother and two sisters of normal height who still live in Germany."

Kurt, Frieda, Hilda, and Elly Schneider were born in Germany to parents who both stood about five foot five. "We were in the Eastern Zone," says Tiny. "Now that belongs to the Russians."

After Kurt and Frieda came to America with a friend, Bert Earles, in 1916, they took his last name. A few years later, sisters Hilda and Elly followed and moved to Pasadena to be with their siblings, also changing their names.

"After Mr. Earles died, we wanted to be on our own," Tiny says. "So we changed our name to Doll because they said we looked like dolls. Kurt is Harry Doll, my name is Elly but I became Tiny, Frieda became Gracie, and Hilda was Daisy."

Harry Doll appeared in the 1930 film *The Unholy Three* with Lon Chaney, as the pseudobaby. He and his sister Daisy also starred in the 1932 M-G-M cult horror flick *Freaks*.

The Dolls were a close-knit family who lived, ate, and worked together. In 1938, while working for the Ringling Brothers and Barnum & Bailey Circus, they drove their car from Sarasota, Florida, to California to appear in *The Wizard of Oz*.

Harry was cast as one of the Lollipop Guild (on the right), while the women were Munchkin villagers.

"We had a nice time in the movie," Tiny, the youngest of the family, remembers. "We liked Judy Garland. She talked to us a lot. And they had such a beautiful set. That's what I remember."

Tiny was twenty-four years old when she was a Munchkin. She says that Harry was the shortest of the family ("not quite three and a half feet") and Gracie was the oldest.

After *The Wizard of Oz*, the foursome drove back to Florida, where they worked for the circus, singing, dancing, and entertaining as parade performers until 1956, when they retired. The four continued to live together, and none of them ever married.

Gracie Doll died in November 1970, Daisy died on March

16, 1980, and Harry on May 4, 1985. Tiny Doll resides in the home she shared with her brother and sisters in Florida.

Alta Stevens Barnes is from Minnesota. She's seventy-five years old and almost didn't make it into *The Wizard of Oz*.

"When our group got to Hollywood, they told Grace Williams and I that we were too tall," Alta says. "I was about four foot five at the time." (She's grown only an inch since *Oz*.) Luckily, when the studio realized they would need all the little people they could get, Alta and Grace were finally hired as Munchkin villagers.

Alta's married to Roy Barnes, and both are now retired. They have one child and one grandson, with another grandchild on the way. Presently, they live in the Los Angeles area.

Reflecting on her career, Alta says she's proud that she worked for the San Francisco World's Fair in 1939 as the mistress of ceremonies at the Midget Village. Her bit parts in other movies include *The Magnificent Ambersons*, the 1942 film directed by Orson Welles, and *Beyond the Blue Horizon* with Dorothy Lamour.

Alta still remembers the wonder of her *Oz* days. "You'd walk on the set in the morning, and you thought you were dreaming. Everyone at M-G-M was so nice to us. They were all friendly."

Emil Kranzler, who played a Munchkin villager, was with the Harvey and Grace Williams group when they headed out to California. Emil performed with them for three summers after *Oz*, then returned home to his family's farm.

"I used to be able to pick myself out," he says of his annual witnessing of the film on television.

Emil is in his second marriage. His wife, Marcella Porter, also a little person, performed when she was young. Now retired, they live in Tempe, Arizona. Emil, who stands four foot six, says he was another of the Williams troupe "who just about didn't get in." Now in his seventies, he repairs bicycles part-time, but he doesn't know how to ride one, he says. He and Marcella are active members of the Little People of America.

When asked what his strongest memory of *Oz* is, he answered, "I really got screwed good when I did *The Wizard of Oz*. I think I only got twenty dollars a week. I was bashful then, and it was the first and only movie I ever played in."

When *The Wizard of Oz* call came to him, **Garland (Earl) Slatten** heartily welcomed the offer to do a movie, since he and his roommate, Harry Monty, were living in Chicago and both out of work. "We were both on skid row at the time," he admits hesitantly. "It was hard for us then, because small people sometimes can't find jobs." His height in 1938 was three foot six, but he's grown to four foot ten now, almost out of the classification of midget.

Earl has portions of two fingers missing on one hand. They were blown off in an accident involving dynamite caps, he says. "I tell kids today that it happened from firecrackers, so they won't be so foolish as to play with explosives when they're young."

Born in Walters, Oklahoma, Earl was twenty-one years old when he marched the yellow bricks at M-G-M as a soldier. "Half of 'em were out of step"—he laughs—"but not me. One time I moseyed over and talked to Margaret Hamilton. It was just small talk, but I remember it well. She was a very nice lady. . . . Also, it was torture trying to eat with that fish-skin on your face. It makes your face stiff. I didn't like that."

After *Oz* he joined the Dolly and Henry Kramer group of performing midgets and worked for a few years on the road. Today he is retired with his wife at their brand-new home in Sequim ("It rhymes with swim"), Washington. He enjoys his status as a Munchkin and can hardly believe it was all so long ago.

Lewis Croft, also known as Idaho Lewis, came from—you guessed it—and he still lives there. He was born in Shelley, Idaho, but now resides in Idaho Falls with his wife.

Lewis stood three foot eight when he played a soldier in *Oz*, but he has grown to about four foot nine. Touring with the Harvey Williams group, Idaho Lewis was never without his guitar.

After *Oz* he worked in a machine shop back in Idaho. Later he worked for the parks department in his city and the R. T. French Company until his retirement. He and his wife love to travel and usually head down south to Arizona for the winter. Lewis is sixty-nine years old.

As for his stint as a Munchkin, Lewis says, "Meeting all the stars and being with Judy Garland was the most incredible thing. There in California I stayed at the Culver Hotel and roomed with Emil Kranzler. It was a job, and I never in any way thought it would be this big."

Tommy Cottonaro was approached by midget actor Billy Curtis on the street one day in Hollywood. He was out of work when Curtis asked him about joining other little people for *The Wizard of Oz*. Tommy heartily agreed, and thus a Munchkin villager was born.

"I almost didn't get to be in the movie," he says. "Leo Singer told me I was too tall and said they wouldn't need me. But later, at the studio, when some man was asking for all of the little people's social security numbers, I gave him mine too, and they told me I was hired. Weeks later, when Singer realized that I had got in anyway, he just gave me a dirty look."

Tommy's height was then and is now four feet six inches, and he was born in Buffalo, New York, on March 20, 1916. He now lives in Niagara Falls with his wife, Elizabeth, to whom he has been married for thirty-three years.

After *Oz* he worked as a manager for a restaurant; he retired several years ago.

Tommy remembers one particular incident on the M-G-M lot: "Back then, I drove a 1934 Pontiac every day. One day we got out early, and it was raining cats and dogs. I had the privilege of parking on the lot. Mickey Rooney, who was on the lot that day visiting Judy, had jacked up the rear end of my car. It was raining so hard that we all jumped into the car. I started it, put it into gear, and, of course, nothing happened. Mickey Rooney and some others were looking out a window at us laughing."

Betty Tanner, now seventy years old, was approached in New York by an agent who requested that she work as a Munchkin villager. She's from Lynn, Massachusetts, and her height then was three foot eight, but she's increased to four foot three.

Her real name is Betty Toczylowski, but for entertainment purposes she shortened her name years ago. She still resides in Massachusetts and has never been married. After *Oz*, she continued on the road performing and also dabbled in hairdressing. "I'm completely retired now," Betty says. "I don't remember much about the movie. I was one of the shy ones on the set, so I didn't run around taking pictures of myself with others and such. In fact, I don't have any pictures of myself now. My health is good though, and I'm thankful for that."

William H. O'Docharty, usually just called "W.H.," can be easily spotted in *The Wizard of Oz* on the back of the carriage that whisks Dorothy to the town square. Look closely, and you'll see Dorothy turn her head and glance at W.H. while in the carriage. He answers her with a cute smile between his pudgy cheeks.

Oz was W.H.'s second film, directly after his appearance in *The Terror of Tiny Town*. He was three foot six then, but now stands about four foot seven. He's sixty-eight and was born on

September 12, 1920, in the heart of Texas. He now resides with his mom, Lillian, in the same state.

Victor Wetter was born in France and didn't become a citizen of the United States until his marriage to Edna Moffit, also a little person, in 1942. He is about four feet tall and played the captain of the marching army in the front of the Munchkins' parade. He also helps Dorothy into her carriage.

Victor worked many of the world's fairs in the United States during the 1930s and 1940s. He and Edna also appeared in *Northwest Mounted Police*, a Cecil B. De Mille film, in 1940.

Victor, Edna, and friend Alyeene Cumming toured in an act called Tiny Troupers of Hollywood in the 1940s and in other vaudeville productions, such as a comedy-melodrama called *The Drunkard*, with other *Oz* alumnus little people.

In the 1950s, Victor and Edna opened a toy store in New Jersey, occasionally playing elves at Christmas on a huge, decorated set.

Now retired, Victor is eighty-six, and his health is failing. "His memory slips a bit," Edna says, "but he still keeps his good appetite." The Wetters live in New Jersey, where they have been for more than thirty years.

Johnny Leal, born on February 26, 1905, was one of thirteen children. Being the only midget in a large family of average-size children had its problems. One time, the other kids built a makeshift airplane for Johnny and shoved it off a small cliff. The pilot, little Johnny, emerged from the rubble relatively unscathed, but his mother wasn't too happy about the aviation attempt.

Johnny worked as an outlaw in *The Terror of Tiny Town* and as a villager in *The Wizard of Oz*. He continued to make show business appearances at various world's fairs in the United States and also worked for Lockheed Aircraft in the 1950s.

Johnny is under four feet and presently lives in a nursing home in Ojai, California; relatives nearby visit their Munchkin uncle regularly.

Johnny lived with his sister, Rose Leal Ferard, for most of his adult life, until he moved into the nursing home around 1978. There he still gets attention because of his role in *Oz*, despite his confinement to a wheelchair.

August Clarence Swensen was born on December 29, 1917, in Austin, Texas. Four-foot, six-inch August went to Hollywood by train and appeared in *The Terror of Tiny Town* just months before he played a soldier in *The Wizard of Oz*. After his brief stint in the movies, he returned to his native Texas.

In 1945 he married his sweetheart, Myrna Myrle, also a little person. He worked at the Kelly Field Air Force Base for some time while raising their three children, who are of average height. Now August and his wife are grandparents, still living in Texas, outside of Austin. "I still watch the movie every year," August says. "Although I haven't kept in touch with any of the Munchkins since that time."

Joseph Herbst went from Joliet, Illinois, to Hollywood to play the sheriff in *The Terror of Tiny Town* and headed back home afterward. He made a repeat trip just months later for a role as a Munchkin villager.

After *Oz*, he worked in his father's grocery store, but he still kept in touch with a few of the little performers.

Just under four feet tall, Herbst has hit age eighty and still lives in Joliet, but he is confined to his home as the result of a stroke.

Unfortunately, my search for the Munchkins led me to many of the group who had passed away. It is virtually impossible to locate and list the correct death dates of all who have died, but here is the information that I did acquire.

Billy Rhodes, who was also known as Little Billy, was one of the top midget actors in Hollywood during the 1930s and 1940s and had some fifty screen credits to his name. He was forty inches tall when he played the Munchkin barrister in the purple gown next to the mayor ("But we've got to verify it legally . . ."). Little Billy died of a stroke on July 24, 1967, at the age of seventy-two, in his Hollywood apartment.

In the front row of the Munchkin soldiers you can spot **Elmer St. Aubin**. Also called Pernell, after *Oz* he returned to Chicago, where years later he opened a bar called The Midget's Club, with his wife, Mary Ellen Burbach.

Pernell, who was not a midget but a dwarf, was the subject of a nationally syndicated Mike Royko article before his death on December 4, 1987. He was eighty-four years old.

Another one of the few dwarfs used in the *Oz* cast was Munchkin villager **Ruth Smith**. She was raised in Marshalltown, Iowa, and joined Singer's Midgets in the early 1930s, playing the piano and singing.

■■

She was married in 1947 to Albert Kline, who died in 1967. Ruth lived to the grand old age of ninety; she died on September 5, 1985, in Iowa.

Frank Cucksey had one of the most endearing roles in *Oz*. As Dorothy sits in her carriage, two Munchkins approach her and thank her for killing the witch. Frank is the second, in a tan coat, who says, "You killed her so completely, that we thank you very sweetly." He bows and presents Dorothy with a bouquet of flowers.

Cookie, as he was called by friends, was born in Brooklyn. After his role as a Munchkin, he moved to Sarasota, Florida, where he worked for many years as a circus entertainer and was a member of the volunteer fire department. He retired from the fire department in 1978 but was still employed by the Circus Hall of Fame and the Ringling Museum of the Circus, where he was a security guard and gave lectures on exhibits.

Frank died in September 1984, leaving his wife, Anna, and two brothers. When he made *The Wizard of Oz*, he stood three feet, but he grew to four foot two, which was his height when he died.

George Ministeri, a very handsome and well-built little person, appeared as the blacksmith and a villain in *The Terror of Tiny Town* and as the coach driver and a Munchkin villager in *Oz*. He stood four foot five when he married his wife, Mary. They had three children and raised them in South Boston, Massachusetts. George, who also worked as a midget acrobat in his early show business days, died of lung cancer on January 29, 1986.

Gladys Wolff stepped onto a train at Union Station with another St. Louis little person, Gladys Allison, heading for Culver City in 1938. Wolff, who was born in 1911, was four foot three. She was married twice and had no children.

During the last few years of her life, Gladys lived in a nursing home in St. Louis. Ironically nurses wheeled her into a TV room to watch *The Wizard of Oz* just weeks before her death. She reportedly smiled, with a tear rolling down her cheek, as she watched the scene she acted in. Gladys died on May 14, 1984, at the age of seventy-two.

James Hulse was disenchanted with show business after his brief stint as a Munchkin villager. This wasn't his line of work, he told relatives. Born on March 16, 1915, in Circleville, Ohio, Jimmy, as he was called, traveled with the Harvey Williams group briefly before *Oz* and returned home almost directly after working on the film.

He later married and had one daughter. Jimmy was involved in a severe accident at a car dealership, which disabled him for the last few years of his life. He died in Columbus, Ohio, on December 29, 1964.

The sergeant at arms of Munchkinland was played by **Prince Denis**, who was named by circus owners in the Pyrenees Mountains of France, where he was born and worked as a young boy. A somewhat hefty military Munchkin, he carries a sword and marches in front of the soldiers. You can also spot Little Denny, as friends called him, in the loft waving his sword at Dorothy as she skips out of Munchkinland.

Denis died on June 21, 1984, at the age of eighty-four, in Phoenix. He had been living in a nursing home for the last few years of his life.

His wife, **Ethel Denis**, drove with him from San Antonio, Texas, to California to be cast in *Oz*. Ethel, who played a Munchkin villager, died in 1968, at the age of seventy-four, in Phoenix. They had no children.

Another husband-and-wife team from Munchkinland was **Johnny Winters** and **Marie Winters**, who legally went by the last name of Maraldo. Johnny acted as the commander of the navy in Munchkinland, according to M-G-M records. Marie, who was Munchkin Prince Denis's sister in real life, was a Munchkin villager.

In 1979, Marie, who was born in France and stood forty-one inches tall, died in San Diego. Johnny reportedly passed away in the mid 1980s.

Nicholas (Nicky) Page, a Munchkin soldier, died on August 18, 1978, in San Francisco.

Franz (Mike) Balluck and **Josefine Balluck**, brother and sister, both returned to their homes in Vienna sometime in the 1940s. Josefine died in 1984, and Mike died on January 24, 1987.

Walter Miller, known to many little people for his ever present spectacles, died on October 26, 1987, in Long Beach, California.

Yvonne Moray Bistany, who played the Munchkin Lullabye Leaguer on the right, was born on January 24, 1917. She worked in Earl Carroll's Vanities vaudeville extravaganza and danced in other vaudeville productions. She starred as the female lead and love interest of Billy Curtis in *The Terror of Tiny Town*. According to friends, she died in the 1970s.

For many years **Billy Curtis** was known as one of Hollywood's most active midget actors. Born in Springfield, Massachusetts, he was forty-five inches tall when he played one of the city fathers in the mayor's entourage in Munchkinland.

Billy came from a family of six children (his sister Mary is also a little person). He was attending Northwestern University in the early 1930s. Then he was, as he said when I interviewed him during the research for this book, "yanked into show business."

He started in two-reelers, and later starred as the hero in *The Terror of Tiny Town*. Billy also appeared in such motion pictures as *Lady in the Dark*, *Saboteur*, *Little Cigars*, *Meet John Doe*, *Friendly Persuasion*, and *High Plains Drifter*, the last opposite Clint Eastwood.

Billy was married three times; his second marriage was his most publicized in Hollywood; this match was with Lois DeFee, a showgirl nearing six foot eight, but it was annulled after three years.

Billy Curtis passed away from a heart ailment on November 9, 1988, at the age of eighty. At the time of his death, he was living in Nevada with his wife, Joan.

A DIFFERENT KIND OF MUNCHKIN

In the film, they're barely seen. Look closely in the background and in the windows of the Munchkin huts. That's them.

Who else could match the size of the midget Munchkins but children? The studio decided to audition and cast nearly a dozen small children to play the background Munchkins, so areas of the set wouldn't appear sparse. After all, this was supposed to be a whole city, and the number of midgets was not as great as M-G-M had hoped for.

"I was delighted to find people who were older than I was and shorter than I was," says Betty Ann Bruno of her experience as a child Munchkin. "I'd run around and measure myself against the midgets sort of surreptitiously. I'd put my hand even to the top of their head and, hopefully without them knowing it, bring it over to my ear. I guess it gave me a sense of stature."

Betty Ann Cain, now Bruno, was born in Honolulu but raised in Southern California. At the time of *Oz*, she was an eight-year-old student of the Bud Murray Dance Studio. She had already briefly appeared in one motion picture, *The Hurricane* with Dorothy Lamour, in 1937. Her mother brought her to the audition for *The Wizard of Oz*, and she was chosen by the dance director. ("We used to call him Cowboy," she says.)

Betty Ann went on to major in political science at Stanford University and now, at age fifty-seven, she is a news reporter, a seventeen-year veteran of KTVU-TV, an Oakland, California, station. She remembers some *Oz* things vividly, as probably any young child in such an elaborate production would.

"I remember the beauty of the set," she says. "It was like going to fairyland every day. And the gorgeous, big plastic flowers. The colors and the vividness. It was magic. I was in awe of that."

Rehearsal for the children first required learning some easy dance steps and a few of the simpler songs, all apart from the midgets. Then the children were measured for costumes just like the other Munchkins—brassieres not included. Except for age, the biggest difference between the children and the midgets was their working hours. The children could work only four hours per day; then it was off to the studio school for tutoring.

"I hated the school, because it was so boring and it was never the same things we were doing in our regular school," Betty Ann remembers. "We always worked on those yellow paper tablets, and I wasn't used to that. The teacher was Mrs. Carter, and, as it turned out later, one of my college roommates was her daughter. Funny how little circles turn around."

Betty Ann also recalls her costume. She wore a gray felt skirt and a little rosebud vase on her head. "I envied everyone else's clothes because they were bright colors," she says.

Betty Ann's mother, Mary Ann Kalama, had the delightful experience of going to the studio every day with her daughter, passing the many midgets while they were getting their makeup put on and drinking coffee before the day's shooting. She recalls, "There were about nine youngsters selected to fill in the midgets. The girls were well taken care of on the set. They didn't allow us mothers on the set, but they had two nurses who accompanied them to lunch and the rest room and helped dress them. It was a very strict rule that the mothers didn't interfere. And the studio treated us mothers nicely. They paid for all of our lunches."

Kalama tried not to be the stereotypical stage mother, so she fully trusted the studio nurses, and little Betty Ann seemed to enjoy the whole unusual experience, including being away from her regular school.

"I do remember this one little girl, Valerie Shepard, because her mother was really a pushy stage mother," Betty Ann adds. "Her mother made Valerie's hair look like Shirley Temple's with curls and dyed it blonde. We'd always look at Valerie's roots. I've always wondered what happened to her."

The memory that Betty Ann has most indelibly stamped in her mind is that of a midget who approached her in a pleasant manner. "There was this guy who kept asking me out to lunch and asking my mother if we could eat together," she remembers laughingly. "My mother would quickly clutch me to her side. One day he asked me what my favorite candy bar was, and I told him it was an Oh Henry! bar. After that morning, we'd kind of muster in a room and then go back to the stage as a group. The midgets would always file by our group, and this one would find me and hold up this Oh Henry! bar, waving."

Being a Munchkin was no ordinary thing. And even more extraordinary was that Betty Ann was a child at the time.

"I've always loved the memory of being on the set and being a Munchkin," she confides. "About fifteen years ago, people here at work found out. It was like I had achieved a separate status. It's a very special thing, and I've just begun to get a glimpse of that. I feel very privileged to have been a part of it."

Joan Kenmore was only seven years old when she was cast as a Munchkin. Born November 3, 1931, she says she vaguely remembers being in the little huts on the set.

"We used to bring out little lunch boxes and eat in those little huts," she says. "One time a little friend and I didn't want to come out of the hut for the scene, but a little midget in the hut with us said he was gonna snitch on us, so we went."

Joan was a member of the Thomas Sheehy Dance Studio when she was cast in *Oz*. A cousin to actor Jackie Cooper, she speculates, "Many of us little kids got the parts because we knew someone."

Now living in California, she revels in her memories of *Oz*. "I remember we got paid eight dollars and nine cents each day," she says. "We'd go through a little booth like the extras and pick up the money. I remember this because my mother put the eight dollars away and always let me keep the nine cents in my pocket for candy."

Like all the Munchkins, neither Betty Ann nor Joan became rich from her work in the film. Nor did they get to keep anything, such as their costumes. M-G-M didn't allow that. They just have their memories to enjoy. "I tried many times to get an auto-graphed picture from Judy Garland," says Betty Ann. "It was frightening. I'd go up to her trailer and knock on the door and ask for a picture. I remember screwing up my courage every day. When I asked, she'd look down at me with those great big eyes and she'd say, 'I'm sorry, I don't have a picture today. Can you come back?' That was very emotional. I did finally get her signature in a little autograph book."

Mayor Mania

4

Munchkinland must have held many elections, because the question of who was mayor has caused such an uproar among Ozologists that the ballots had to be closely examined. However many candidates there may have been for the highly rated position mayor of Munchkin City (". . . in the county of the land of Oz,") there was only one bona fide mayor.

For the past fifteen years, who held this position has remained a mystery because of conflicting claims, misreportings, and a lack of available M-G-M documentation. The man who played this green-suited, whiskered, chubby Munchkin who sported an oversized gold pocket watch died relatively unknown in the early 1970s in Oakland, California. His name was Charley Becker.

Seemingly the most popular of the inhabitants of Munchkinland, the mayor has received enormous amounts of media coverage in the past ten years, coverage that would have made Becker gleam with Munchkin pride. Unfortunately, Becker's name was never connected with any of these stories, which involved others who claimed to be the jolly welcomer of witch quenchers. Perhaps they felt that nobody would ever know the difference since there were so many little people in the movie. The real one, however, is unmistakable. Charley Becker was Leo Singer's right-hand midget.

Becker was born on November 24, 1887, in Muschenheim, Germany (a small town near Frankfurt), and given the name Karl Becker. He worked as a butcher and a sausage maker before he was recruited by Baron Leo Singer to be part of a traveling midget troupe around 1918. He married his second wife, Jessie Kelley, after meeting her on the set of *The Wizard of Oz*, where they both worked as Munchkins. (He already had a son by his first marriage.) On July 23, 1943, Becker stood in front of a judge in Oakland, California, and became a U.S. citizen. According to the *Oakland Tribune*, when asked what he thought of Adolf Hitler, Becker responded, "Ugh, I don't want to even hear his name!"

Becker, three feet, nine inches tall and known by the other midgets as "a terrific cook" (according to Nita Krebs), was also a favorite of his boss. Singer took special care looking after his core group of midgets and ensured that Becker would receive a prime role, just as Nita, another of his favorites, was placed well as one of the Lullabye League.

Becker also played the cherubic cook in the movie *The Terror of Tiny Town*. Being a competent actor made his job as mayor of Munchkinland quite easy, although, according to an August 1939 *Good Houskeeping* article, he had prepared himself for an engineering career. When writer Jane Hall visited the movie's set during production, Becker remarked to her, "Nobody takes an engineer seriously these days, I mean if he's also a midget."

Although Becker was a part of the midget entertainment world for most of his life, when he died he was given no celebrity-status funeral. He had been in his eighties. But the spirit of the mayor of Munchkinland refused to die, and false news stories about this favorite *Oz* character continued to pop up everywhere.

The Associated Press released a story on June 23, 1984,

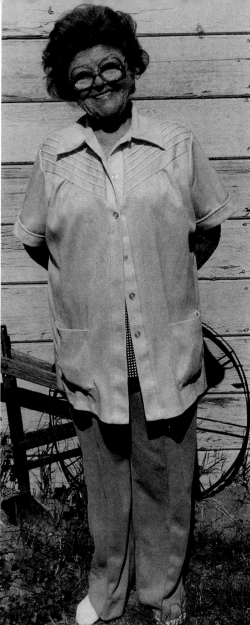

LEFT: "America's Tiniest Bombshell of Song," as Dolly Kramer was called, now enjoys her retirement in Miami Beach. *(Photo by Stephen Cox)* RIGHT: Now living in California, Jeanette Fern, a.k.a. Fern Formica, a.k.a. Johnnie Fern McDill, who was one of the youngest of the Munchkins. *(Photo by Stephen Cox)*

PRECEDING PAGE: Publicity shot of a group of Leo Singer's midgets inside a normal-size refrigerator. Left to right, back row: Christie Buresh, Nita Krebs; middle row: Freddy Ritter, Eddie Buresh, Jackie Gerlich; front row: Karl Slover, Jeanette Fern. *(Courtesy of Fern Formica)*

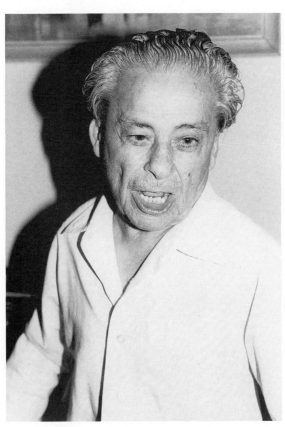

ABOVE: Harry Monty, who played a Winged Monkey as well as a Munchkin soldier. He lives in Hollywood. *(Photo by Stephen Cox)* TOP RIGHT: Emil Kranzler, as he looks today in Arizona. Retired, he now repairs bicycles. *(Photo by Stephen Cox)* RIGHT: Ruth Robinson Duccini in her Arizona home, 1988. *(Photo by Stephen Cox)*

OPPOSITE: Johnny and Marie Winters riding high on the hog after having played Munchkins. RIGHT TOP: Johnny Leal sued and won a case against Jed Buell Productions for the scar on his cheek that he acquired from his makeup when acting in *The Terror of Tiny Town*. He played a villager in *Oz*. *(Courtesy of Johnny Leal)* RIGHT: Johnny Leal in a shirt that's a bit too big.

ABOVE: Nita Krebs, the only living Lullabye Leaguer, as she looks today at her home in Florida. *(Courtesy of Nita Krebs)* RIGHT: Nita Krebs as a ballet dancer before the making of *The Wizard of Oz. (Courtesy of Nita Krebs)*

ABOVE: Karl (Karchy) Slover, no longer the smallest one of the bunch, has grown almost a foot since 1938. He is now living in Florida, where he trains dogs. *(Photo by Stephen Cox)* RIGHT: After his stint in *Oz*, Munchkin Frank Cucksey worked for twenty years as a lecturer on exhibits at the Ringling Museum in Florida. *(Courtesy of Anna Mitchell)*

ABOVE LEFT: Idaho Lewis Croft holds the original soldier vest he wore during the movie. A fan from Kansas owns the tiny, stitched piece of history, which Lewis admits wouldn't fit anymore. *(Photo by Stephen Cox)* LEFT: August C. Swensen at his home in Texas, in August 1988. *(Courtesy of A. Swensen)* ABOVE: Robert Drake and his wife of more than forty years, Jeane LaBarbera. Little Jeane, as she is known, and her husband are retired and living in Florida. *(Photo by Stephen Cox)* OPPOSITE: Husband-and-wife team Robert Drake and Little Jeane LaBarbera in a publicity still taken during their heyday. *(Courtesy of Robert Drake)*

Murray Wood, dressed to kill.
(Courtesy of Murray Wood)

Munchkin Alta Stevens in 1988, with her husband, Roy Barnes, and their grandson. *(Courtesy of Alta Stevens)*

LEFT: Eight-year-old Betty Ann Cain was cast as a Munchkin although she was not a midget. She was one of nearly a dozen children who played Munchkins and remained in the background of the scene. RIGHT: Betty Ann (Cain) Bruno, a television news reporter in Oakland, California, in 1988. *(Both courtesy of Betty Ann Bruno)*

ABOVE LEFT: Gladys Wolff in St. Louis, shortly before her death in 1984. *(Courtesy of Pat Jordan)* ABOVE CENTER: Victor and Edna Wetter in 1986. *(Courtesy of the Wetters)* ABOVE RIGHT: Billy Curtis, one of Hollywood's most famous little people, shortly before his death in late 1988. *(Courtesy of Jerry Maren)* BELOW: Just months after completing *Oz*, Little Billy Rhodes made his second appearance with the Three Stooges, in their two-reeler *You Nazty Spy*. *(Courtesy of Columbia Pictures)* OPPOSITE: Singer's Midgets pose for a publicity shot during a U.S. tour.

A series of four-inch porcelain statuettes by the Franklin Mint features three of the Munchkins and a Winged Monkey. *(Courtesy of the Franklin Mint)* OPPOSITE, LOWER RIGHT: These adorable Munchkin dolls now available in toy stores are popular items for *Oz* fans. Multi Toy offers a set of five different Munchkin dolls in addition to replicas of the main characters. Left: Munchkin soldier. Right: Munchkin mayor. *(Courtesy of Multi Toy Company)*

Many of the midgets walked to work in the morning, since their hotel was just blocks from the studio. An unusual sight—even for Hollywood! *(Courtesy of Margaret Pellegrini)*

that was picked up in virtually every large city in the United States. "The Mayor of Munchkinland, Dead at 84" headlines read. The only problem with the story was that the actor who actually played the mayor had died approximately ten years before. The man who died in 1984, Prince Denis, had been a Munchkin, but not the mayor. The story was not alone; additional reports appeared which placed the "real" mayor in Atlanta, Hollywood, and New York.

Denis lived in a Phoenix nursing home, where for many years he boasted to his nurses, friends, and even the press that he had portrayed the mayor of Munchkinland. His chubby appearance, like that of Becker, would have made even the most ardent Ozologist glance twice.

In actuality, Denis played the hefty sergeant at arms, who led the soldiers and waved to Dorothy from atop a hut when she exited Munchkinland. If you look closely, you can see that Dorothy even gave Denis a wave back. The mayor he was not, yet fans of *Oz* mourned the mayor's passing when Denis's death was publicized.

"[Mervyn] LeRoy chose me for the mayor's role because I was the heaviest character of the bunch. He thought I appeared the most distinguished," Denis told a Phoenix newspaper in 1980. Because of his portly build, he felt that nobody would mind or contradict him if he said he had been the mayor.

"*I* knew he wasn't," says Margaret Pellegrini, fellow Munchkin and friend of Denis in Phoenix. "But I didn't want to be the one to point the finger and say he wasn't. He told me he was the second choice for mayor, but he knew he didn't play it. We all knew Charley Becker for years. I was a roommate with his future wife, Jessie, when we made *The Wizard of Oz*, so there's no mistaking who played the mayor.

"Denny received a lot of attention that made him feel very good during his last years," Pellegrini explains. "But I didn't like covering up for him. I avoided the subject in interviews. Once I had to tell people at the TV show '60 Minutes' not to come out to interview us when they called me because I didn't want to lie about the mayor."

My subsequent research produced documents as well as photographs proving that the real mayor had died years earlier. And what a term he held! Charley Becker can finally be recognized as the true mayor of Munchkinland. If he were alive, he'd probably get reelected in a landslide vote. But watch out for those impostors!

Three Alarm in Munchkinland

5

"Like hell it was fun," Jack Haley said to inquisitive *Oz* fans about his role.

Originally, Buddy Ebsen was cast as the Tin Man and he held the role well into the third week of filming. But he fell severely ill and was hospitalized for ingestion of the silver makeup, which coated his lungs. He was replaced by Haley, a fine decision without a doubt. But like his predecessor, Haley detested the makeup and costume.

Some film productions, especially those involving special effects, seem to be plagued by accidents. For instance, a fire, injured cast, and other mishaps held up filming of *The Exorcist* for weeks; *The Wizard of Oz* was a similar case. Calamities started at the beginning, and an accident in Munchkinland on December 23, 1938,* could have taken the life of one of film history's most

*An M-G-M memo of January 5, 1939, records December 28, 1938, as the day of Hamilton's accident. This date seems erroneous, based on my research.

convincing evil entities: the Wicked Witch of the West, actress Margaret Hamilton.

The scene we see in the film was the first, and most successful, take. The Munchkins' celebration of the death of the Wicked Witch of the East is interrupted by the startling intrusion of her sister, the Wicked Witch of the West. The stunt involved Hamilton's double, Betty Danko, coming up through the floor (on somewhat of a catapult, as Danko and Hamilton both described it in interviews) with her back turned. Then the shot was stopped, and Danko was replaced by the wickedly convincing Hamilton. The appearance is preceded by a burst of fire and red smoke.

Hamilton screeched her lines and departed through the same hole, but her exit had to be done without a cut or a stand-in, so Hamilton practiced to make sure her cape, broom, and body would not be a hindrance. "Perfect!" yelled Victor Fleming. Lunch was called. The second take, after lunch, proved detrimental to Hamilton's health.

For director Fleming, another take of the same scene was necessary to ensure that it had been effectively captured on film. This time, before Hamilton had sunk on the little elevator, the fire and smoke were triggered prematurely; flames engulfed her face, hair, and hands. Her costume and broom had ignited, but she didn't realize the emergency until she was mobbed by technicians rushing to her aid.

"Somebody yelled, 'Get somebody, she's burning!' " remembers Jerry Maren. "Members of the crew and others were running up to the floor area."

Another Munchkin has a different memory: "Something the public doesn't realize is that just out of camera range was a fireman with a soaking, wet blanket," says Meinhardt Raabe, Munchkin coroner. "The only damage she sustained was singed eyebrows and melted makeup. She was back on the set the next day and had no serious injuries."

Actually, Hamilton was sent home and did not return to the production for nearly six weeks. Since that particular shot was her last for the scene, none of the Munchkins saw her after that nearly catastrophic day. Her injuries were worse than anyone envisioned.

"When I looked down at my right hand, I thought I was going to faint. That's when the pain really took hold," Hamilton said later. "The fire had singed my eyebrows off and burned my cheeks and chin. At first I had just felt some warmth on my face, and I didn't realize what had happened."

Because of the raw skin, which left her hands quite fragile and fleshy, Hamilton wore slick green gloves in lieu of the copper-containing makeup for the remainder of the movie.

Most of the Munchkins vaguely remember the incident. Some of them have even described valiant rescues they performed, saving Hamilton's life. Hamilton told reporters before her death in May 1985 that she did not remember any Munchkins coming to her aid.

Ironically, days before the accident, dance director Bobby Connolly made an urgent announcement asking all the little people not to step on the witch's trapdoor and to watch their movement around this area.

Munchkins Nita Krebs and Garland Slatten recall that just minutes after the announcement Connolly stumbled into the hole and landed on the shoulders of stand-in Betty Danko. Later, Danko recalled the mishap, also mentioning back problems she suffered from Connolly's unexpected plunge.

"We laughed when he fell," says Slatten. "He had just told *us* to watch it!"

6

"It's Going to Be So Hard to Say Good-bye"

It was the close of 1938. Christmas was over, and with the approach of a new year came pleasant visions of returning home. The Munchkins were dismissed from their contracts on the evening of December 28. Some of them were already packed, with their train tickets resting on their readied suitcases.

But before the last day was up, M-G-M's front office sent urgent word to the studio that none of the Munchkins would be cleared to leave the city until a matter with Leo Singer was resolved. Production staff were in a mild frenzy over Singer and his sudden impulse not to cooperate with the studio's final shooting.

Keith Weeks, the production manager, had informed Singer the day before that he would require twenty of the little people to stay an extra day or so for retakes, photographs, and any other last-minute details. Singer refused, claiming he knew nothing about such requirements.

The M-G-M legal department quickly reviewed Singer's contract and highlighted the clause that referred to holding the whole group in Culver City. Singer was informed that unless it was honored the Munchkins' final paychecks would be held.

When Singer signed his contract with Loew's Incorported, part of the agreement clearly included keeping the entire group in the city for two weeks after completion of filming in case M-G-M required retakes. But Singer did not think that M-G-M would enforce this clause, and he refused the services of any of the midgets.

Weeks immediately contacted the legal department, and they hurriedly instructed him on how to handle the situation before the ensemble had wrapped for the day.

Late in the afternoon on that last day of shooting, Weeks quietly entered the studio, staring at the tired midgets in costume and makeup. Victor Fleming was also worn out. It had been a long six and a half weeks.

As the final "Cut" was heard from Fleming's permanent perch on the camera boom, Weeks gathered the Munchkins around him and thanked them for their performance. "At this time and in Singer's presence, I recalled to the set to work the following day approximately 20 midgets," Weeks wrote later in a memo. "I stated also that all the other midgets were definitely closed on the picture, but that [Singer] would be paid for the 20 midgets pro rata for whatever time I would need them."

Weeks purposely mentioned the financial addendum aloud so the remaining twenty little people would not be alarmed about compensation. Obviously, Singer had not told any of them about an extended stay; however, he finally agreed, although adamantly complaining about Weeks delivering the announcement rather than himself. Apparently, Singer felt uneasy about retaining only twenty and dismissing the rest.

"I remember staying for those days when the others had left," says Fern Formica. "It was a lot of us smaller ones. We took some still photos, and one of them is the shot where Glinda and Dorothy look into the bushes and Margaret [Pellegrini] and I are peeking out."

During the added two days of work—Thursday, December 29, and Friday, December 30—the twenty Munchkins filmed the sequence where they race after Glinda's pink, glistening bubble rising over Munchkinland. Waving and bouncing, they look upward and yell "Good-bye, Good-bye" at virtually nothing, since the bubble was inserted by the special-effects department later, during editing.

Across town during the same two days, many of the little people were weaving in and out of crowds trying to get to their track at the Los Angeles train station. Just like Dorothy in the movie—excited yet sad—they were going home, bursting with memories.

At the Culver Hotel, many of the little people said their good-byes and promised to keep in touch along their travels. The All American Bus Lines driver screeched the door closed as his group slumped in their upright seats. This time, the bus would tread through snow and wintry conditions, returning the little people to their hometowns along the way.

Other midgets were going back to work with their vaudeville troupes—directly into the next engagement. Still others loaded their cars and headed home, anxious to tell their families about working in something new . . . a color motion picture.

They were movie stars.

"And, Oh, What Happened Then Was Rich!"

7

It was the year of unusual film phenomena, with studios unleashing such blockbusters as *Gone with the Wind*, *Wuthering Heights*, *Goodbye, Mr. Chips*, *Mr. Smith Goes to Washington*, and *Ninotchka*. Incredible competition.

Oddly enough, the "great spirit" of *Oz* did not triumph until nearly twenty years later, when the movie was aired on television. When originally released, the film did not even recoup the expense of its production. It actually lost money. By its popularity today, you'd never know it.

M-G-M never had such a turnaround. *The Wizard of Oz* as a property faired quite well over the thirty years after its television debut November 3, 1956, on CBS. Presently, Turner Broadcasting owns the film, after their landmark purchase of many of M-G-M's holdings, including *Gone with the Wind*.

Interest in *Oz* has really never diminished. It gave the actors—all of them—their most famous roles and put Munchkins on the map.

Oz-related celebrations, reproductions in many forms,

books, theater screenings, and merchandising have escalated the popularity of the motion picture into a class all its own. Moreover, the American Film Institute in 1978 voted it the third best film in history.

"Who would have thought it would do so well?" says Munchkin Mickey Carroll. "When I heard about the movie, I thought, 'What the hell is *Wizard of Oz*? What is the Lollipop Guild?' It was like gibberish. I wasn't familiar with the children's book at the time."

Now the Munchkins are the only members of the cast who can personally promote the movie. Frank Morgan, who played the Wizard, died in 1949; Bert Lahr, the Cowardly Lion, died in 1967, Judy Garland, in 1969; Billie Burke, who played Glinda, the Good Witch, in 1970; Jack Haley, the Tin Man, in 1979; Margaret Hamilton, the Wicked Witch, in 1985; and Ray Bolger, the Scarecrow, in 1987. It is possible that extras who portrayed the Winkies (the witch's soldiers) or the green-clad inhabitants of the Emerald City are alive, but so far none have surfaced publicly.

It looks like the Munchkins will be doing a solo on the Yellow Brick Road from now on. But thanks to countless organizations and activities and, naturally, the appeal of the film itself, Oz will survive in hearts for generations to come.

Luckily, society has accepted little people much more than it did when *The Wizard of Oz* was conceived. Despite certain limitations, little people can achieve a success equal to or even greater than that of average-size human beings. Today their options have expanded, and they are able to explore opportunities in all facets of life. Despite many hindrances, a number of the actors who played Munchkins followed their yellow brick road to successful careers and healthy families, and they have one thing that no others have—true memories of *Oz*.

Keeping the legend of the film alive is actually easy, since so many are willing to undertake the job—especially the Munchkins. It doesn't take much . . . only a willing heart. And proof that the legend won't dwindle lies in society's reflection, the marketplace, the Oz trading post.

THE OZ PHENOMENON

Here's just a smidgen of the Oz-Munchkin fanaticism:

■ A 1977 book, *Murder on the Yellow Brick Road*, by Stuart Ka-minsky (St. Martin's Press). This is a cute tale about a Munchkin who has been murdered on the set of *The Wizard of Oz*. A detective hired by Louis B. Mayer tries to unravel the mystery and keep Judy Garland and M-G-M free from scandal. Of the tome *The New York Times Book Review* said, "It's all very nostalagic and rather sweet. It's all good, clean fun; and when the film buffs finish reading it, there will not be a dry eye in the house."

■ In Chittenango, New York, birthplace of *Oz* author L. Frank Baum, an annual celebration each May of his books and the motion picture enchants the town and hundreds of visitors.

■ The Yellow Brick Road Gift Shop put Chesterton, Indiana, on the map. Near Chicago, Chesterton is the location of an annual Oz festival around Labor Day that plays host to several Munchkins and gets the whole town involved in Oz activities. The gift shop, open all year, includes a Wall of Fame with autographed photos of the cast, a replica of the witch's castle on the mountain, and more. "It's a fantasy museum," says owner Jean Nelson. "Like a grown-up toy shop."

■ Dunkin' Donuts, a leading chain around the United States, introduced their Munchkin "donuts" in the early 1970s. Actually, the little snacks are bite-size donut "holes" whose original boxes are cutely adorned by tiny chefs passing giant pastry pieces down an assembly line. Today Munch-kins are still a popular item among morning munchers and can be purchased in bulk loads.

■-■

■ The International Wizard of Oz Club, in operation since 1957, publishes a slick magazine, *The Baum Bugle,* to satisfy its more than two thousand members. Conventions are sponsored each year in varying locations for aficionados to meet other serious students of Oz. Interested readers can obtain information by writing The International Wizard of Oz Club, Box 95, Kinderhook, Illinois 62345.

■ Dorothy's House, in Liberal, Kansas, has a sign that says it is the "Gateway to the Land of Ah's." This extensive museum has duplicated the Gale home in Kansas and boasts as its prize piece the original miniature model house used in the movie (twirling down the twister in a special effect). Conventions and celebrations have amassed crowds from around the country at the site, where you can have your name engraved in a yellow brick for posterity. The movie is shown daily, with groups of six or more required for a screening.

■ The Mego toy company marketed a Munchkinland Playset in 1974, complete with a mayor Munchkin doll and its own carrying case. Additional Munchkins sold separately—as did an Emerald City Playset and The Witches Castle Playset. Just in time for *The Wizard of Oz's* thirty-fifth anniversary, this was one of many merchandising items that faired well that year. Each play set now fetches up to $250 among collectors.

■ In more recent years, footage cut from the original film has been available to the public. The 1984 M-G-M/UA film *That's Dancing!,* with Ray Bolger as a guest host, premiered an excellent dance sequence by Dorothy and the Scarecrow that was cut from the final *Oz* print. In addition, rare home-movie footage—a "jitterbug" musical sequence—from the collection of one of the film's songwriters, Harold Arlen, was presented on TV's "Ripley's Believe It or Not." This was believed to have been cut because it dated the motion picture (as if the farmhouse scenes don't date the film at all!).

■ In 1981 Orion Pictures released a fantastic flop, *Under the Rainbow*, which portrayed the Munchkins of Oz as drunkards, rowdies, and whores. Critic Leonard Maltin says, "Even by today's standards, this is an astoundingly unfunny and tasteless comedy about spies, undercover agents, and the midgets who cross paths in a hotel during the filming of *The Wizard of Oz*. Is this film the Wicked Witch's revenge?" This movie increased fans' love for the original and made people angrier about the inflated rumors concerning the Munchkins.

■ Merchandise based on the movie, its characters, and the Munchkins has been incredibly wide ranged. Posters, stationery, board games, collectors' plates, paper products, wallpaper, pillowcases, bubble bath, soundtrack albums, puppets, dolls, miniature figurines, buttons, Hallmark greeting cards, postcards, play sets, T-shirts, Halloween masks, and ruby-slipper necklaces have been dangled in the market. Hucksters do well by their Oz mementos, and the fans purchase more each year. St. Louis's Elaine Willingham runs a mail-order business, appropriately named Beyond the Rainbow, which supplies Judy Garland material to buyers and collectors.

■ The Franklin Mint, of Franklin Center, Pennsylvania, has produced a line of extraordinary porcelain sculptures in intricate detail of the cast of *Oz* to celebrate the film's fiftieth anniversary. Twenty figures in all, these beautiful four-inch, hand-painted characters represent every scene of the film. Naturally, Dorothy, the Scarecrow, the Tin Man, and the Cowardly Lion all have statuettes. So does the mayor of Munchkinland, one of the Lollipop Guild, one of the Lullabye League, and even a fearsome Winged Monkey. These are available exclusively through the Franklin Mint by direct mail. In several years, pieces such

as these become eagerly sought collectors' items among
Oz fans.

■ Munchkin dolls manufactued by the Multi Toy Company of
Cresskill, New Jersey, hit the market in late 1988. The
seven-inch rubber figures include a mayor, a Lollipop
Guild Munchkin, a Lullabye toe dancer, a soldier, and a
female Munchkin villager. Sold in individual boxes, this
Oz doll line offers eleven-inch replicas of the film's main
characters as well. "They look a little dwarfish," says
Munchkin Margaret Pellegrini about the Munchkin toys.
"But that's OK. They're cute, and so are their costumes."

Undoubtedly, *The Wizard of Oz*'s following is large, has endured
for decades, and will exist for hundreds of years to come. The
Munchkins have finally arrived. Recognition for them is belated
but certainly due. They might have gotten the short end of the
stick when they received their paychecks, but the residuals are
the fans. And the Munchkins will have fans forever.

Metro-Goldwyn-Mayer presents
A Victor Fleming production

THE WIZARD OF OZ

The Cast

JUDY GARLAND	Dorothy Gale
FRANK MORGAN	Professor Marvel/Wizard
RAY BOLGER	Hunk/Scarecrow
JACK HALEY	Hickory/Tin Man
BERT LAHR	Zeke/Cowardly Lion
BILLIE BURKE	Glinda, the Good Witch
MARGARET HAMILTON	Miss Gulch/The Wicked Witch
CHARLEY GRAPEWIN	Uncle Henry
CLARA BLANDICK	Auntie Em
PAT WALSHE	Nikko [head Winged Monkey]
TERRY	Toto

and THE MUNCHKINS

DIRECTED BY Victor Fleming
PRODUCED BY Mervyn LeRoy
SCREENPLAY BY Noel Langley, Florence Ryerson, and Edgar Allen Woolf
ADAPTATION BY Noel Langley
FROM THE BOOK BY L. Frank Baum
MUSICAL ADAPTATION BY Herbert Stothart
LYRICS BY E. Y. "Yip" Harburg
MUSIC BY Harold Arlen
ASSOCIATE CONDUCTOR: George Stoll
ORCHESTRAL AND VOCAL ARRANGEMENTS:
George Bassman, Murray Cutter, Paul Marquardt, and Ken Darby
MUSICAL NUMBERS STAGED BY Bobby Connolly
PHOTOGRAPHED IN TECHNICOLOR BY Harold Rosson, A.S.C.
ASSOCIATE: Allen Davey, A.S.C.
TECHNICOLOR COLOR DIRECTOR: Natalie Kalmus
ASSOCIATE: Henri Jaffa
RECORDING DIRECTOR: Douglas Shearer
ART DIRECTOR: Cedric Gibbons
ASSOCIATE: William A. Horning
SET DECORATIONS BY Edwin B. Willis
SPECIAL EFFECTS BY Arnold Gillespie
COSTUMES BY Adrian
CHARACTER MAKEUPS CREATED BY Jack Dawn
FILM EDITOR: Blanche Sewell

Running Time: 101 minutes

About the Author

Steve Cox graduated from Park College in Kansas City, Missouri, with a B.A. in journalism and communication arts. Steve, a television and movie historian, has contributed to six books about the high priests of low comedy, The Three Stooges, and he is the author of the TV book *The Beverly Hillbillies*. He is five foot six.